THE BITING POINT

Catherine Smith

speechbubble *books*

THE BITING POINT

First published in 2010 by Speechbubble Books
24 South Way, Lewes, East Sussex BN7 1LU
www.speechbubblebooks.co.uk

ISBN 978-0-9567306-0-2

British cataloguing in publication
A CIP record for this book is available from the British Library

Cover photograph: Istockphoto
Printed in Great Britain by Lightning Source

For my sons

CONTENTS

Every Seven Seconds   8

The Kettle   20

What a Girl Can Make and Do   32

House Hunting   44

The Castle   54

Thomas   60

Fridays   70

Sow   80

The Ascension of Mary   94

Reclamation   104

The Bear   116

The Biting Point   122

EVERY SEVEN SECONDS

Yesterday afternoon I watched Mr Crawford try to kill himself. I'd climbed over the fence into his garden to get my ball back. I'd just started on a new Extra Strong Mint. I heard noises coming from his garage and I went in. He was crying and trying to tie a rope over the beam in the roof. He had snot all over his cheeks, like the glaze on the top of a pork pie. He kept saying, 'Bugger off, lad. Just bugger off.'

But I didn't. I stayed and watched.

Today at the meeting with Mrs Palmer, Mum keeps twisting her hands into a ball, like she's winding string or something. It's hot in the room and a bee keeps bashing its head against the glass. Mrs Palmer's mouth looks like a cat's bum, all pursed and angry and pink. I want to push a pencil into it, to watch it grip the sides. If you shove something up a cat's bum, Darren Waters says, it grips on with its muscles and goes rigid. That's how the vet takes a cat's temperature, but you can do it just for a laugh. Their eyes go huge as saucers, according to Darren. They're too surprised to scratch you. They go into a trance.

Darren knows lots of things.

'It's mainly a question of attitude, Mrs Page,' Mrs Palmer says to Mum, tapping her nails on her desk like she's bashing out a message in Morse code. 'He doesn't pay attention, doesn't apply himself to his work, and he often disturbs the other pupils. He's not stupid, by any means. In fact in many ways he's very bright. Aren't you, Billy?'

I slump in my chair and make my eyes go blank behind my glasses and open my mouth so a tiny stream of dribble collects on my lower lip. Mum shoves me in the side.

'Things have been very difficult,' she says. She speaks louder and faster than other people. 'Since his Dad left home. He's found it very hard to adjust.'

Mrs Palmer's mouth. A pencil, or maybe a stick. The muscles going rigid, clamping on. Or a piece of iron, a bit rusty. The way her pupils would grow huge. The way her eyebrows would shoot up. She'd be paralysed.

'And the truanting,' Mrs Palmer says, frowning at Mum. 'As you know, our rules state quite unequivocally...'

Mrs Palmer uses big words because she thinks they frighten people. Useless with me and Mum. Mum's been to university and reads the *Guardian* and Mrs Palmer with her cat's-bum mouth and long words can't scare me.

On the way home on the bus, Mum looks out of the window and sighs. I keep my head down in case anyone sees.

'Mr Crawford,' I said. 'What are you doing, Mr Crawford?'

He looked at me like I was stupid. Most people think I am stupid because the lenses in my glasses are like jam jars and I'm small for my age and I don't speak that much.

I don't speak that much because it seems to me most people speak when there's nothing to say. They speak to convince themselves they're still alive.

He was crying loudly, like water going down a drain but getting stuck. I've never seen a man cry, not properly, only at football matches on TV and that doesn't count because it's put on. They get paid more if they cry, another thousand pounds a minute sometimes. Darren told me.

'I'm going to kill myself, you little git,' he snivelled. 'Now bugger off.'

It was weird in his garage. There was no car and everything was really tidy, shelves of jam jars with paintbrushes in them and newspapers tied up with string and old oil cans all stacked up. There were dead bluebottles belly-up on the workbench and patches of petrol on the floor. The smell made my head ache.

He was muttering to himself, coiling a rope around his arm and trying to swing it over the beam in the roof. It was difficult for him because he was snivelling so hard and shaking and every time he tossed the rope it fell short and then he started cursing. He ignored me for ages and then he said, 'Well, don't just stand there, lad. Get a chair. Go and fetch a chair.'

I went round the side of the house and let myself into the kitchen. It was the same size and shape as ours but it didn't have piles of papers and clothes everywhere or yesterday's washing-up all over the table. It stank of disinfectant and all the surfaces were clean and tidy. On the table there was an envelope addressed 'To Whom It May Concern' in neat capital letters. I dragged a chair back round to the garage.

He climbed up on it and got the rope over in one go. That seemed to cheer him up.

'Right,' he said. 'That's sorted. Now bugger off, for God's sake.'

I leaned against the wall. He was mopping at his face with this great big hanky with his initials on. R.C.C. He was wearing a black suit and his face was bright red.

'Why don't you take your jacket off, Mr Crawford?' I asked

him. His neck was red and sort of bulging with veins, like a bag of snakes. He was frowning, standing on the chair and working on the knot.

'This is none of your business,' he snapped at me. 'Go on, get out of it.'

Nothing is ever my business. Mum and Dad screaming at each other was none of my business. Mum crying after he left. Empty gin bottles behind the toilet. Final reminders from the power companies. Why other people had Dads. Inside my Mum's bedside cupboard where she keeps books with pictures of naked people and plastic things and tubes of gel and stuff.

'You can't make me,' I said. And he looked at me right in the eye and I felt something like an electric shock go through me and I started smiling and I couldn't stop. 'Can you?'

This afternoon Mum tries to talk to me about school. She gets out my old reports and spreads them all over the floor, like they were Christmas wrapping or something. The ones from infant school where they said I was 'challenging' and had 'difficulty relating to other children'.

What I remember about my first class was a big cupboard where the teacher kept all her papers and paints and stuff. When no one was looking I used to crawl in there and curl up and put my arms around my head and just listen to the others running around like maniacs and singing songs and stuff, or playing at kings and queens and building castles. Like they mattered.

'All right, have it your own bloody way,' Mr Crawford said, shuffling his feet on the chair. He put the rope around his neck – he'd tied it into a noose – and started taking these big, noisy breaths. He scrubbed at his nose with his hanky and sniffed a lot.

'Perhaps I should say a prayer,' he said, not really to me, more to himself. 'Asking forgiveness. For the inconvenience. For the unclean thoughts and everything.'

'Do you believe in God, then?' I asked him. No one I know really believes in God, only teachers, and they're probably pretending because we all have to be quiet during prayers so they get a few minutes to think about something more interesting, like sex. Darren says all teachers think about sex every seven seconds. Sometimes you can see it on their faces, when they sort of glaze over and look out of the window in the middle of explaining something really boring, like similes or photosynthesis.

'Of course I believe in God,' he said, and got down off his chair. 'Here, you might as well join in, while you're here. Kneel down.'

The garage floor was cold and damp and we stayed there for ages. Mr Crawford had his hands clasped together and whispered things. I didn't pay much attention. I know there isn't a God and even if there is, he's not much use because he doesn't stop bad stuff like wars or my Dad leaving. I was wondering when Mr Crawford would get back on the chair and how long it takes to hang yourself, whether you'd hear the neck snap or anything. Darren told me that people who get hanged shit and piss themselves and they have a huge hard-on that never goes down.

'Right,' he said at last, wiping snot across his face. 'That's that done. Now I've made my peace. With the Lord. Now I've asked forgiveness for my sins. I can do it now.'

'What were they?' I asked him, helping him to re-position the chair.

'What?' he snapped, glaring at me.

'Your sins,' I said. 'What were your sins?'

He plonked down on the chair. The top of his head was shiny and pink. One of his ears stuck out more than the other one.

'Young girls,' he whispered. 'In the park, when I come back

from visiting Mother. She lives in Alberry Villas, you see, she relies on me. She's eighty-seven. I visit every day. She's on her own, very independent. She's a wonderful woman. I never let her down.'

I thought he might go on about visiting his mother, which I didn't want to hear. I know about visiting old people; Mum makes me visit my Nan once a month. She smells of orange squash and Dettol and she sits with her legs open because her knees are all swollen, so you can see her horrible fat thighs. Her teeth don't fit properly, so when she kisses me it's like a jellyfish sliming my cheek.

Mr Crawford sat gazing into space. He didn't seem to know I was there, really. Then he said suddenly, 'Young girls out walking. Wearing hardly anything, showing their tits and their bellies and their arses. Tempting me. I'd wait behind trees, when it got dark. I'd watch them. They'd be shivering a bit, in the cold, but they wouldn't cover up, oh no. And I'd watch them from behind my tree and I couldn't help myself. I'd find myself holding it. You know. Stroking the tip. Warm, getting firm. Watching their arses wiggle and the flesh on their bellies firm and hard and listening to them laugh.' He looked straight at me. His left eye had a tiny burst blood vessel in the corner, like a red spider. 'They laugh at old men like me, girls do, but I know what's what. I'm not finished yet. I can still get it up.'

His breathing was so loud I thought his chest would burst open. He washed his hands in the air and his knuckles were white and hard.

'They didn't see me, and I never said anything to them. I just watched them. I wasn't doing any harm. Except the last time. Friday.' He started shaking. 'She was one of those half-caste girls, skinny. Tight jeans. You could see the shape of her cunt in them. No knickers or anything. She wanted it. Not from me, oh no, not from an old man, from some young bloke. She wanted him to hurt her. I couldn't help myself. I called out to her. I said, "See this? Suck this, you little tart." Then I ran off. But she heard me, you see. She heard me. Now they'll find me and the shame will kill Mother...'

All the time he was talking I kept staring at him. He got redder and redder. The words he used – arse, cunt, tits, bellies – made my stomach go tight and hard. Down there I got hard too; I could feel it straining against my pants. Harder than ever before. Fantastic. I couldn't take my eyes off his face.

Now Mum's putting the reports away and sighing a lot and asking me what's making me unhappy. She doesn't wait for me to answer – she just says I'm obviously behaving like I do because I'm sad about stuff. Only she doesn't say stuff, she says 'issues'. She's started saying 'issues' a lot since she's been going to see her counsellor. She says I'm emotionally young for my age.

No I'm not. I'm nearly thirteen and I know what Mr Crawford did in the park and how it made him feel and why he wanted to die. Nobody else knows that.

'How about family therapy?' she asks me. 'You know, we could go and talk to somebody who understands about children and families and you could explain what makes you unhappy.'

Yeah, right. Somebody in a grey cardigan in a grey room with a cat's-bum mouth who wants to peel the top of my head open and take a good look at my thoughts. Somebody who probably thinks about sex every seven seconds.

I pick my nose and pretend not to listen.

'You're not going to do it, ' I said to him. 'You're not going to kill yourself. Are you, Mr Crawford?'

He sat with his head in his hands and cried.

'I don't have the guts,' he moaned, wiping his nose on his jacket sleeve so it looked like a snail had wandered across. 'I don't even have the guts to kill myself. I'll have to turn myself in. I'll have to tell the police. Now that people know.'

'Only me and that girl,' I pointed out, unwrapping another Extra Strong Mint and putting it under my tongue so the taste went into the bottom of my mouth, the way I like it to. 'And she might not say anything.'

'That's true,' he sniffed, scrubbing at his eyes with his hanky. 'She hasn't so far. She knows, you see, she knows what I said to her was true. She wanted me to say those things. It turns them on, these girls, they get a kick out of it.' He started crying again. 'I only did it to show her where she was going wrong. I've done her a favour, really. I've shown her the error of her ways. If she goes round dressed as a tart, men will take advantage, she'll have a dog's life. She should be grateful to me.'

I transferred the mint from under my tongue to the roof of my mouth. I made noisy clacking noises because Mr Crawford seemed to have forgotten me; he was muttering to himself.

'And you, lad,' he sniffed, standing on the chair so he could untie the knot and get the rope down, 'you wouldn't say anything, would you? Eh? Our little secret. Man to man.'

'Well,' I said, sucking hard on the last of my mint and staring him full in the face as he coiled the rope around his forearm, 'that depends, Mr Crawford.'

Mum gets on the phone to Dad and it's one of those conversations where she shouts and her eyes go like tiny black pin-points and her neck goes rigid. She looks like she used to look when he lived here.

'You have to take some responsibility,' she yells. 'I can't handle him on my own. You don't know what it's like, constantly up to the school with that sanctimonious cow of a teacher looking down her nose at me. I've got my own life, you know, not that you bloody well care. You're not providing a proper role model for him, you never come when you say, you're behind with the maintenance…'

I kick the skirting boards six times but she doesn't notice. I go up to my room.

'I've nothing to give you, lad,' Mr Crawford said miserably, as I made the tea in his kitchen. He'd taken off his jacket; there were dark stains under the armpits of his white shirt; I could smell his sweat. There was no milk – the fridge was empty – but I found some chocolate biscuits in the back of a cupboard and dipped one in my tea and sucked the chocolate off and he didn't moan at me, like Mum would. 'It's no good asking me for money. I've got my pension and that's it. I'm not saying I'm poor, but there's none left over.'

Suddenly I felt angry, angrier than I've felt since Dad left, angrier than when Darren laughed at me in the swimming pool because I couldn't handle breathing underwater and kept sort of drowning, angrier than all the teachers in the world have ever made me. *Fuck you, fuck you*, I wanted to shout, because adults always say they can't give you anything – money, sweets, respect, trainers, a Dad, a fishing trip in a boat with mackerel wriggling on the floor, games for your Game Boy. I remembered the last time my Dad took me to Alton Towers and he ran out of money and we couldn't have cokes in the cafe. 'I'm sorry, Billy, I can't buy you everything you want.' I'm sorry, Billy, but you're an ugly little sod with thick glasses and hardly any friends except Darren Waters and he's going to get excluded soon anyway. I'm sorry, Billy, but I can't be bothered to stick around and watch you grow up because I'd rather spend my money on someone prettier than you and younger than your Mum who doesn't moan at me all the time.

'I want something!' I shouted, banging my mug down so the tea splashed on his clean blue tablecloth. 'I want you to give me something. Something of yours.'

I tried not to, but I was crying. I hadn't cried for over a year and it hurt my throat and my nose wouldn't stop running. Somehow it didn't matter, crying in front of him; I didn't want him to like me or respect me or anything.

He looked at me, sort of surprised, and stroked his straggly little moustache and then his eyes glazed over.

'Well,' he said, 'there's some reading matter. You might find it... educational.'

Then we went upstairs to his back bedroom, which had the curtains drawn and stank of furniture polish. There was a crappy bronze crucifix on the wall, with Jesus looking miserable. Mr Crawford hauled out a battered brown suitcase from under the bed and undid the leather straps. He sat back and let me look. It was full of shiny magazines with girls pointing naked bits of themselves at me. They had their lips and legs open and it was like they were saying, *Come in, come in, you're welcome.* They had perfect skin and shiny hair and whiter-than-white teeth. They looked at me straight in the eye; they had their fingers between their legs, and their tongues curled round their top lips. I thought of the words Mr Crawford had used. *Tits, bellies, arse, cunt.* They rolled around my mouth like my Extra Strong Mint.

'You're welcome to these,' he said, not looking at me, loosening his shirt collar. His hands were shaking. 'I'm moving out of this area. Then I won't have to cross that park, I won't have to see those... girls. Better for Mother if I sell up and move in with her, see she's looked after properly. It's the sensible solution.' He cleared his throat. 'I'll find you a bag or something, lad. I won't be needing these any more.'

This evening, Mum calls Dad on the phone and for once she doesn't yell, she talks in this subdued voice and then she hands me the receiver. This time he actually bothers to speak to me and he says he's coming to family therapy with me and Mum to 'help me get sorted'. I don't say anything. I can hear music in the background, his girlfriend's music, his young girlfriend Lisa with the pointy tits and a way of looking at me like I'm something she found on the bottom of her shoe. He's obviously waiting for me to be grateful and glad, like the puppy-dog he wants me to be, wagging my tail and saying yes, Dad, thank you, thank you for remembering me, while he's really like all the teachers, thinking about sex every seven seconds. I know he's hardly even listening because he's thinking about Lisa and what they're going to do with their clothes off.

I put the phone down on him when he's in midstream, banging on about our 'relationship' and what it means to him and how one day I'll understand why he had to leave. I already understand. I understand about women's bodies, I know the way they make you feel, the way you can't stop thinking about them even if you want to, the way he feels about Lisa so he wishes I'd disappear into a hole in the ground so he can spend all his time with her.

I know all these things and he can't do anything about it. I even know more than Darren Waters, though I don't spout my mouth off like he does. I go upstairs and wedge a chair in front of my door and take out Mr Crawford's magazines from under my bed, with those women all shiny and beautiful and open, and what I know is this: they're waiting for me, waiting just for me.

THE KETTLE

Five days after your lover dies, the kettle stops working.

Your husband stands by the work surface, pushing the orange button. It won't engage, clicks out again immediately. He tuts. He's late, hungover, and in urgent need of coffee.

'We haven't had this very long, stupid bloody thing,' he grumbles. 'Can you get one today? I won't have time.'

'No problem,' you say, watching the way he tucks his blue striped shirt into his trousers. He's put on weight and his belly bulges over the waistband. Before your lover died you'd have found this secretly, shamefully revolting; your lover was slim, lithe, and for a long time you've no longer found your husband desirable. On the rare occasions you've fucked him, you've closed your eyes and thought of your lover's body, of the taut belly, the biscuity scent in the crooks of elbows and knees. Now, watching your husband slosh orange juice into a glass, you find you don't have an opinion about his body, one way or the other.

'Have you spoken to Fran?' he asks, wiping his mouth.

'Yes.' You think about her voice, like gravel crunched under-foot – the rawness, how she sounded scoured. The silences.

'How's she doing?' he asks, shovelling cornflakes into a bowl.

You hate him then, actively hate him. You hate him for asking the questions that everybody asks, perfectly reasonable and totally idiotic. You hate him for leaving all the contact up to you, assuming that because you're a woman you'll do and say the right things. Above all, you hate him for not knowing that you'd loved Fran's husband for three years, for not guessing how much you'd like to go back to bed, pull the duvet over your head and howl.

'How do you think? She's in bits.'

'The funeral will probably help,' he says, with his mouth full. 'Poor cow.' Little bits of bright orange cereal fleck his chin. He eats heartily. The noise sets your teeth on edge.

'Don't forget,' he says, scraping his spoon around the bottom of the bowl. 'Kettle.'

You go to Argos in your lunch hour. All morning it's rained, a warm rain, and the pavements are greasy. You flick through the catalogue's bright pages until you come to the household-appliances section. The kettles are mostly chrome, and they gleam like highly-polished trophies on immaculate faux-marble worktops. Some have in-built water filters; some are environmentally friendly. One or two are transparent and remind you of goldfish bowls; you shiver as you think of a goldfish jumping the waves of boiling water, frantic, dying.

You note down the catalogue number of the cheapest kettle and stand in a queue behind a man who taps his foot impatiently. You wonder what that feels like – impatience, urgency. You can't imagine. You feel as though you're underwater most of the time, as though everything's slightly blurred and you're waiting to take a really deep breath. And surface.

'Would you like to take out extra insurance with that?' asks the sales assistant. 'Covers you for loss, damage...'

'No thanks,' you say, handing her your debit card. 'There's no point. They never last that long anyway.'

At three o'clock, you ring Fran.

She sounds exhausted but calm. The autopsy's complete. Death caused by massive trauma to the chest and head. No sign of drugs or alcohol in the body. Possibly he fell asleep at the wheel, he'd been working really long hours... You cluck, sympathetically, and she sighs. The funeral's on Monday, there's a notice in the local paper.

'How's Josh?' you ask.

'Up and down. Sometimes it's like he's perfectly normal, you know, gets all his Lego out, wants crisps when he's watching his DVDs, all the usual stuff. But he's been sleeping with me at night, he can't stand being alone. Nor can I, actually, so I'm letting him. Some nosy health visitor will probably say I'm storing up trouble but they can fuck off. It's nice to hear somebody breathing next to you in bed. All that warmth, you know?'

'Yes, absolutely,' you say. 'I know.'

'How's work?' she asks.

'New campaign. Hell,' you say lightly and then after you've each said, 'Bye now, take care', you hate yourself for saying work is hell. What a stupid, insensitive thing to say. Work is just work, a way of getting through the day. A way to go on living.

On the way home you lose a black leather glove. You realise this just as you're through the turnstile at Tooting Bec, where you always pull them on, and you feel panicky and sick. You stop abruptly, just where you are, and people sigh as they skirt round you. Searching bags and pockets, you wonder where it fell. It's fine Italian leather, supple and pliant, smelling faintly of Amarige, bought two years ago in Harvey Nichols, at your lover's suggestion.

You remember when you wore the gloves and nothing else. The heat from the gas fire in the hotel room in Huddersfield scorching your thighs, the nylon rug scratchy under your skin, and the way his cock stiffened instantly when you drew the gloves on to your hands. You remember how gratifying that was, knowing that just the sight of your hands in black leather could produce such an impressive hard-on. You remember how his eyes locked on to yours as you pumped and pumped, how he called you a delicious little slut. His semen, white and glutinous, like albumen, pooling on the black leather. How sweet it tasted, like coconut. How you wondered if it would stain the leather. It didn't.

You give up searching after a few minutes, knowing it's gone. You place the remaining glove in a wastebin near the station, on top of greasy chip paper and a battered Special Brew can.

Walking home, on pavements still steaming slightly, you long for a bath. One of the local street drinkers, a woman dressed in a man's sweater and grubby tracksuit bottoms, asks you for money to buy tampons. Her face is puffy and puce, her hair's dry as Styrofoam but her eyes are electric blue, unexpectedly beautiful, and they burn into you. You wonder how she got here – she's probably only your age, early forties. You wonder what it must be like to be hunched in a shop doorway and feel your belly spasm like a fist opening and closing inside, to feel warm blood trickling down your legs.

You hand her a £5 note, your last one. It's a stupid, over-the-top gesture but it makes you feel, momentarily, better.

'You're looking good, Mary Jane, you old slag,' shouts a man with filthy shoulder-length hair and a shivering lurcher.

'Fuck off, yourself,' the woman shouts back then leans forward, looks you straight in the eyes and says, 'God bless you, darling, God bless you for your kindness,' and you catch her feral scent.

You wonder if she once had a lover or a husband, or both; kids, a job, decent clothes. Good gloves.

When you get home, the butter and milk from breakfast are still on the kitchen table and your fourteen-year-old son is playing his bass guitar so loudly the whole house shakes. You quite like that; you can feel the beat rising up through your feet, jangling your teeth and bones.

You shout 'Hello!' up the stairs, as loud as you can. His door opens and he shouts, 'When's dinner?' *Dinner!* The thought of cooking turns your stomach.

You shout back, 'Shall we get a takeaway?' And he shouts, 'Yeah, cool. Chinese.' You think what a crap mother you are, failing to plan meals, cook, make face-to-face contact with your only child.

You stand in the kitchen and peel the plastic off the new kettle's box and leave it on the work surface. You ought to unpack it properly, plug it in, fill out the guarantee form and find a stamp.

But you don't want tea or coffee anyway.

You fix yourself a large gin and tonic. Since your lover died, you've found most food and drink tastes of nothing, you can barely distinguish between flavours. But gin and tonic, with that sharp, quinine kick, that aftertaste, brings your tastebuds to life.

You drop two ice-cubes into the glass. They crack, and the tonic fizzes again. You take a sip and decide it needs lemon. As you're slicing through the skin with the blunt vegetable knife, juice spurts out and the cuticle on your left index finger stings like crazy. You automatically bring it to your mouth and suck, hard, and your eyes fill with tears. You hadn't noticed that miniscule cut, that treacherous little bastard waiting for the lemon's acid to find it out.

When your husband comes in you're on the sofa in the living room, on your third gin. You like to feel it growling in your guts.

'Morphy Richards?' he asks, as though it's a question you should answer, sensibly. He plants a kiss on your cheek. His breath smells of red wine and cheese-and-onion crisps. His eyes are still bloodshot. Since your lover's death, he's been drinking more. He only knew your lover socially, as your friend's husband, for barbecues and men's curry-and-beer nights, but as he said when it happened, it makes you think. A bloke who was barely forty, fit as a flea, one wrong move on the motorway, wiped out.

'Wasn't the last one Morphy Richards? Weren't there any other makes?'

You look at him and have no idea what he's talking about.

That night when your husband comes to bed, you pretend to be asleep. Once he's snoring and grunting, you lie awake for hours, watching the car lights strobe the ceiling. When you fall into uneasy sleep at 3am you dream you're driving along a dual carriageway and your lover is a passenger in a car passing the other way. You catch a glimpse of his face: the dark hair, aquiline nose, crescent-shaped scar on his chin, caused – and you've always found this detail tender – when he fell off a shed roof when he was seven. In the dream you cry out, call his name, but the car's already gone, hurtling away in the opposite direction, a blur of silver metal. You couldn't see who was driving.

Next morning you weigh yourself and find you've lost five pounds. You know you shouldn't feel pleased about this, but you do. Already your trousers hang looser on your hips and your belly is flatter. You trace your ribs under the skin. You lift a handful of loose flesh from your left buttock and squeeze, thinking of how your lover described your arse as 'grabbable' and how, occasionally, he'd slap it during foreplay, leaving the stinging red imprint of his fingers. The first time he did this you were shocked, slightly embarrassed, but the next time, you liked it. You liked the sudden thrill of the pain, the way the skin tingled and smarted, the intimacy of it. The trust.

You'd like there to be less of your arse, now he's not here to appreciate it. You want there to be less of you, altogether. You step into the shower and turn the water on, hot and fast. You like the roaring sound, the water running over your mouth. Showering with your lover was a delight, the press of his hard, wet stomach against yours, the mat of dark, curly chest hair, the salt of his skin under your tongue.

You like the fact you can cry in the shower and no one can hear.

After you've towelled yourself dry you realise your mouth feels as though a small creature died there overnight – and, as you're cleaning your teeth, there's an even more horrible taste. You realise you've squeezed John Frieda Frizz Ease Flawless Finishing Crème on to your toothbrush and you spit and rinse, vigorously. You find yourself laughing and think, for a second, how your lover will laugh and say you're an adorable fuckwit when you tell him about it.

Before you go to work, you make sure your husband and son are downstairs, then you shut the study door and check your Hotmail account. Your lover was the only one to have this address. You haven't looked at it since the day before the crash. You've wanted to – you wanted to immediately, to read the message that said, hey, it's fine, it's all been a stupid mistake, I'm still here.

You type in your password – sexfiend, his pet name for you – and there it is, his last message. 'Well, fucking Manchester overnight then Fran's birthday, we're out for a meal at Gianni's apparently, so I guess it's Friday at the earliest – can you wait that long, gorgeous? Can we meet at Victoria, 6pm? I've got something for you, a little toy I think you'll like. Stay sexy, N xxxxxxxx'

You sit and stare at it for almost a minute. He died on her thirty-ninth birthday. Driving at – what? – eighty miles an hour? – down the M1 to be with his wife. His wife, his little boy. His family. Of course, what else could he do? Meetings had gone on longer than expected, he'd left a bit late, he'd really had to put his foot down. A momentary lapse of concentration. A misjudgement, the newspaper report had said. Uncharacteristic. Normally a very competent driver.

You delete the message – you've always deleted his messages, just as you've always deleted his texts from your mobile phone – and start to cry. You visit it again, in the trash can. You re-read every word, try to imagine his smile as he was typing it – hurriedly, at work. It was sent at 11.15 a.m.

By tomorrow it will be gone. The last of him will be gone.

A present. A toy. He liked to buy you presents. You have a secret stash of dildos, leopardskin split-crotch knickers, clit gel, handcuffs, wrapped in a Monsoon bag at the back of the top shelf of your wardrobe. You wonder what you'll do with them now. You think about what he'd say. Find another lover, gorgeous, or you could always hand them in at the Oxfam shop. Anyway, fuck it, they're only things.

You check the new emails on your Yahoo account. Several offer you cut-price Viagra for a better, more satisfying erection. One suggests you could buy yourself a degree from an American university. Four are about his death, one from a woman you and Fran used to go swimming with. 'I can't take it in,' says the message. 'I read about it in the paper and suddenly realised who it was. Nick. All that life-force and energy. And he adored Fran and Josh. It's awful.'

You type a reply, agreeing that your lover adored his wife and son, agreeing that it's all a terrible shock. No flowers, donations to Cancer Research. His mum had breast cancer. He lost her when he was quite young, so Fran thought – and then you find yourself sitting back and staring at the screen. You've no idea what Fran thought, how thoughts could form and be articulated in the violence, the chaos of all that grief.

Your husband knocks, opens the door and hands you a mug of Earl Grey tea.

'Good kettle,' he says, touching your cheek. 'Really good kettle.'

'Good,' you say and smile, and try to mean it.

On Saturday night you drink a bottle of Pinot Grigio and toy with the Sainsbury's Fisherman's Pie and watercress salad. Your son disappears after eating some of the fish and none of the salad. Your husband asks for seconds, and devours two large bowls of mint-chocolate ice-cream as well. You watch *The Madness of King George* on DVD. At the point where the king is running along a corridor in his nightshirt, terrified and roaring, your husband turns to you and asks if he's got a black tie.

The day of the funeral, the weather's hot with a brilliant blue sky – an Indian summer September day after weeks of muggy drizzle. The weather strikes you as wrong; it should be dull, overcast. You're sweating in black; you keep your sunglasses on. Your arms are burning and you remember the first time your lover commented on the fine golden hairs on your forearms – one of your early meetings, a lunchtime drink at a pub in the city. Gently flirtatious conversation, until he kissed you goodbye and you realised, as you pressed against his body, that he had an erection.

Fran and Josh, and your lover's brother, sister and her husband, arrive at the crematorium chapel as you make small-talk with friends in the carpark. You notice that Josh is clutching a Lego helicopter and decide you will take him some new Lego later this week. Your husband – in a suit slightly too tight and a black tie borrowed from a neighbour – smokes a cigarette. Your son scuffs his shoes on the concrete and looks bored.

The coffin, shouldered by four sweating men, gleams in the bright sunshine. You can't believe he's in there.

You're aware you're on the B-list of mourners. You file in after Fran's family, her closest friends, her sisters, brother, parents, nephews and niece. The chapel is full – your lover's work colleagues, old friends from school. You sit near the back.

'We Have All The Time In The World' seeps from the speakers. You shiver and your husband pats your knee. Your lover once said to you, after a boozy night in the city when you were supposed to be out with 'the girls', that he wanted this song at his funeral. 'It's the irony,' he said. 'Because by that time, there'd be no time, would there? I'd have snuffed it.' You told him you thought it was sick.

The service, conducted by a short, stout vicar you think looks like the Fat Controller, is a blur. You focus on your shoes, black leather, polished that morning. Too officey, you think, too flat and sensible. Your lover didn't like them.

When Fran stands up, the curtains close, and she presses the button under the coffin and the electric motor starts up and you know his body is trundling towards the furnace. You let the tears slide down your face into your mouth; some drip off your chin and you're paralysed, you can't wipe them away. Your husband dabs at his left eye with a handkerchief his mother gave him for Christmas five years ago – and then passes it to you. You press it against your face. It smells musty.

You would give anything in the world at this moment to smell your lover's skin.

Two weeks later, at nine in the evening as you're on your third drink, Fran rings. She's laughing.

'I don't believe this, I just don't fucking believe this!' she says. 'It's so... weird. I'm having some wine actually. Shouldn't, but – you'll never guess what's happened.'

Your heart stutters. You put your glass down, your hands shaking. It's a mistake, the whole thing. She's laughing because it's all been a mistake. It wasn't him. He's alive. He's back.

'What?' you ask.

'I'm pregnant!' she shrieks. 'We'd been trying for three years, I'd more or less given up. We'd both had tests and stuff, nothing showed up but with our history – you know – anyway... I thought I'd missed my period because of all the shock and stuff but I did a test yesterday and I've been to the doctors and she's confirmed it. I'm about seven weeks...'

'That's amazing,' you hear yourself saying. 'Oh Fran. Oh, Fran.'

'I'm going for it,' she says. 'It's mad in a way. I mean, here I am, widow, traumatised kid, thirty-nine, but it's his baby, you know? His last gift, the best bloody gift in the world. He always wanted a second one. Oh God, I shouldn't say this, but I really hope it's a girl. He always wanted a daughter, I know he did.'

'Oh Fran,' you say again. 'It's... that's...'

'All that great sex! He'd bought me a new vibrator for my birthday. A black one. Massive. The dirty dog. I found it in his sock drawer. Gift-wrapped. Oh, God, this is so bizarre. You don't mind me telling you this stuff, do you? It's just, you're always so calm – he always said, you're the most sensible friend we've got...'

'No,' you say. 'Course not. I'm glad you did. I'm glad.'

After you've put the phone down your husband opens the living-room door and points at your empty glass.

'Another one?' he asks. 'Or I shall put the kettle on?'

'No,' you say, your voice underwater. 'No. Nothing.'

WHAT A GIRL CAN MAKE AND DO

I can tell by her expression that she's in love, and it's a fierce love, not easily thwarted. She stands squarely, feet apart, squeezing the soft, malleable body in its lemon Babygro to her chest. The head flops back on its slack neck. She stares at the puckered face. She's smitten.

'No,' I tell her, trying to sound firm but kind, and failing. Have I always sounded so tired, so waspish? A month ago, surely, my voice was warm, reasonable?

'But I *need* her,' she says, and our eyes lock. 'I *really* need her.'

'No, Molly, you don't. *Really* you don't.'

I try prising her fingers open; they are locked tight, like a body with rigor mortis. She's got enough dolls, for God's sake.

'You don't need her,' I say. 'You've got Emma and Sophie *and* Rapunzel.'

It's so quiet, our breathing is audible. This is going very badly. Beads of sweat prickle the back of my neck. It's ridiculously hot in the shop, and because it was drizzling when we set out, we're both sweating and scratchy in our waterproof jackets. We're here to buy a present for my brother and sister-in-law's new baby, Adam. Adam is their third child, and already, at a week old, is feeding perfectly and giving them four hours' sleep at a stretch. My brother and sister-in-law clothe their babies in fair-trade cotton and carry them in award-winning slings until they are six months old, and do not really approve of a surfeit of 'material goods' for babies; but if a present isn't forthcoming other members of my family will notice, and disapprove.

Molly has her tongue curled over her top lip and is frowning slightly – both bad signs denoting extreme concentration. I'm aware that the shop staff – a sanctimonious old cow of a manageress with rigid hair and a surly school-leaver chewing the remains of black varnish off her nails – are watching us with interest. We might, possibly, be the first tantrum of the day; it's only ten o'clock, after all. I unzip my waterproof. We might be about to make what my Granny would have called *a Holy Show* of ourselves.

I clear my throat and take a deep breath.

'Molly,' I say, 'we need to put her back now and choose a present for Adam. There's a good girl.'

'I *need* her,' she says firmly, running a finger over the snouty nose. She avoids my eyes. Another bad sign.

'What we *need*, darling, is to buy Adam a present. And we need to do it quickly because we've got lots to do and then we need to have lunch and we need to get you to nursery...'

'I need her for a baby for Emma and Sophie,' she says, hugging the doll tighter and rubbing the toe of her boot on the carpet. '*They* need her.'

'Emma and Sophie don't need a baby,' I say, a touch too cheerfully, dropping down on to my knees so that we're at eye-level. Stress the positive; keep calm and unfazed. The adult should be in charge, should set a good example by their mature handling of challenging situations. 'They've got Rapunzel.'

Rapunzel was originally mine, made for me by my Granny as a present for my third birthday – a cloth doll with a red gingham dress and bloomers and frayed woollen hair down to her ankles. My hair was deemed 'impossible' – always short and kept scraped off my face with vicious kirby grips. Rapunzel's features were sewn with tiny red stitches and her cheeks were pink smudges. My Granny was brilliant at making things. I didn't inherit her abilities, although she left me her sewing box, with its threads and needles, its quick-unpick and its scraps of material and ribbon.

'Rapunzel's old,' says my daughter coldly, turning her back on me and propping the doll's head on her shoulder so it lolls forward and stares at me with its newborn face. 'And she's ugly and I hate her.'

Suddenly I'm yanking the big-headed, soft-bodied doll out of her arms, and Molly's hanging on and screaming so loudly my eardrums vibrate, and we're squaring up to each other like boxers. And fuck it, I really want to knock her down, to get her to submit, apologise, take back that spiteful remark about Rapunzel – to scream into her face, *This isn't fair, this is not a fair fight.*

My mother rings on the dot of one o'clock.

'Am I disturbing you, darling?' Her voice is sweet and reasonable. I stand in the hall, which is draughty and dark, trying not to yawn, holding the phone we always meant to relocate to the kitchen and never quite got round to, and notice how dusty the floorboards look. She'll be sitting by the little gilt-edged table in the hall, her housework completed. The house will smell of lavender polish and plug-in air fresheners. She'll have had a few friends round for coffee, no doubt, where they'll have sympathised with her about my 'situation' and then she'll have had lunch alone, at the kitchen table, listening to Radio 2, while my dad is out golfing, despite the weather, with his retired friends.

'Well, it's Thursday, Mum, so I have to get her to nursery by half past...'

'Oh, is she still going?' That innocent tone, such treachery. 'I thought she didn't like it at the moment?'

Didn't like it was an understatement. Since David left Molly had clung to me like a tree-frog and sobbed every time we approached the building. I had to peel her off me to hand her over to Karen, the pathologically jolly nursery nurse, who assured me, over Molly's wailing, that she'd be fine 'once she was enjoying herself with all her friends'. My grin was a rictus, so forced my face ached for hours afterwards. I'd walk away with her screams ringing in my ears, stop at the end of the road to fumble in my bag for cigarettes and smoke one sitting on the wall, like a skiving teenager – aware that precious minutes available for work were slipping away and avoiding the eyes of the mothers wheeling their placid, well-adjusted toddlers past me.

'She doesn't, she hates it. But if she doesn't go, I'll go mad, and anyway I have a feature to finish and the deadline's today.'

'But if she's *upset*...' murmurs my mother. 'Couldn't she just stay at home and play quietly?'

'No way. She already had a huge paddy in the toy shop this morning. We went for a present for Adam and she wanted this bloody doll.' I could imagine my mother wincing at this, but carried on. 'Which I didn't let her have. We're not actually speaking.'

'Well,' my mother sighs, 'I suppose you have to expect this sort of thing at the moment. It's the shock. I just hope David can live with himself, after what he's done – he is still having her this weekend?'

'Yes.' I pick at a loose thread unravelling from my sleeve. 'Actually, he's having her for three days. He's taking tomorrow off and picking her up tonight, six o'clock. He and the lovely Tashina.'

'Ridiculous name,' she snorts. 'I mean, on top of everything else. What sort of name is *Tashina*?'

'Her mother made it up, apparently.' I remember asking David the same question, when he told me who it was, this woman he loved so passionately and absolutely he needed to move out of our home and into her flat. Tashina, a sales rep from the office. He'd just given me a large glass of wine, half of which I'd gulped down more or less in one, and I blurted out what a stupid bloody name she had, on top of being a home-wrecking bitch.

'From bits of other names,' he'd said, calmly. 'She just liked the sound of it. It's a beautiful name, actually. It suits her.'

'Speaks volumes,' says my mother. 'Anyway, why is he having her tomorrow as well?'

'I'm busy,' I say. I pull the wool hard and it snaps in my fingers. I must stop picking or the whole cuff will unravel. It's a bad habit I've had since childhood – ragged sleeves, chewed collars. 'Deadlines. Lots on. I need to make a living, remember.'

'Yes, well. Have you sorted out the maintenance yet? You can go to court, you know, they can force him to pay. Even though you're not... well...'

'Even though we're not *married*,' I say. 'Yes, I know. But it's not necessary, so far. He's being very reasonable, actually.'

'So far! It's only been five minutes. You want to get yourself a good solicitor. Daddy can give you the number of our man at Henderson's – well, it's a woman, these days, but she's very good, Asian, actually, very *educated* girl...'

'Thanks,' I say. 'I will. Soon. When I need to. Look, I really must go and get ready, get her ready...'

'Well, give her a lovely hug and kiss from me,' says my mother. 'I'll ring you tomorrow.'

'No, you can't.' I crane my neck to peer around the living room door, to see if Molly has mellowed. She's sitting cross-legged on the floor, poker-backed, watching her *Little Mermaid* DVD, her thumb jammed into her mouth, her index finger stroking her nose. 'I won't be here.'

'I thought you said you were working?'

'I am. Not from home. I have to go and interview someone.'

'Well, I'll ring in the evening...'

'No, Mum, don't.' Don't, I think. Not tomorrow. Let me have a day off from your questions, your anxiety, your sighs. 'I'll ring you over the weekend. Tomorrow's tricky.'

The drizzle has turned nasty; now it's a downpour, under a pewter sky. People have switched on lights in their living rooms, making it easy to see in; once I glimpse a mother reading to a child nestled in the crook of her arm, slumped on a sofa. Drains swell and gurgle, and leaves are flattened and slippery on the pavements. Cars spray our legs as we walk along the road in silence – hand in hand, but politely, like children who've been ordered to pair off on a school trip. Lately she's whined as we approached the building but today she's silent.

'You'll have a lovely time,' I whisper, my lips pressed to her ear through her soft shock of hair – 'too fine for anything' as successive hairdressers, and my mother, have informed me. Mine was – is – just as hopeless; she'll never have a fat, glossy ponytail and thick fringe. I unzip her waterproof in the nursery corridor and hang it on a peg underneath a picture she's drawn of a fluorescent pig. Drops of water splash on the tiled floor; we both stare at them. The corridor rings with the sound of clattering feet, raised voices. Molly says nothing. I take her hand and lead her into the main room. Clusters of children swathed in bright plastic overalls, standing in front of miniature easels, gravely splosh paint – mostly a mucky brown – on to paper. The windows have steamed up, and the room smells of overripe fruit.

'Look, Molly,' beams Karen, 'it's painting time! Shall we find you an overall?'

She slips her hand from mine, takes Karen's and walks forward, without a backward glance.

At home I stand in the hall, shivering as I shrug off my soaking waterproof, and wonder what she'll paint. The house is full of her paintings – bright pigs, rainstorms, exuberant babies, stuck to cupboards and walls with Blu-Tack, the edges curling like dry leaves. I've never been able to draw or paint. I look at her portrait of me with my rainbow umbrella, my huge lips grinning red, and know this gift, this joyous, marvellous gift, is something she gets from her father, the cheating bastard. And from her great-grandmother.

My Granny had a book she liked to share with me, a book from her own childhood, with a cracked spine and burgundy cover showing two curly-haired, rosy-cheeked girls threading painted shells on to a piece of wool. It was a book full of resourceful schoolgirls baking gingerbread men for their younger siblings and knitting spectacle cases for grandparents out of leftover wool from old pullovers; a book from a golden age of children who amused themselves productively, whose beds boasted crocheted blankets and whose underwear drawers contained embroidered handkerchief cases and chiffon lavender bags. It was her fond hope she'd teach me to make something from it, that I'd grow up resourceful and artistic like her, not prissy and unadventurous like my own mother.

'Look, butterfingers!' she'd laugh at me, as my papier-mâché piggybank sagged and collapsed. 'More glue, darling!' My mother, passing by the kitchen where we sat at a table piled with strips of newspaper and pots of watery glue, would sigh and tut. 'More mess,' I overheard her say to my father one Sunday morning, 'and it's not as if she'll ever make anything we can actually *keep*. It all goes in the bin.'

A car backfires in the street, and I find I'm still in the hall, in my shoes, the bottoms of my jeans damp and stiff, and I'm cold, and crying, which is useless, useless.

In Molly's room I clear piles of clothes into the washing basket, plump up her pink duvet, remove balled-up socks from under her bed, thump her cushions until they are fat and soft. I open the window and cold, clean air blasts in. When she comes home it will be tidy, tranquil, the staleness gone.

I find her rucksack and pack clothes and night things for three days. Extra knickers – since David left she will, on occasion, stand in the middle of a room, scream, fold her arms and then send a long, clear stream of urine down her legs. Her dolls. Emma and Sophie are easy to find, their plump, smug faces grubby from Molly's rapturous kissing. Rapunzel is nowhere to be seen.

I go through her cupboards – avalanches of toys – and a slow heat rises in my chest. You ungrateful little cow, I find myself thinking as I burrow through piles of Lego, she's no ordinary doll. She's special, every stitch done by hand, not assembled on some fucking production line in some foreign factory by women paid less in a week than I spend on your nursery fees for an afternoon.

And then I find her. Her hair's been chopped off, great jagged cuts. Her body's folded, as though her limbs have turned to jelly. I hold her against my face and breathe her in: calico, spittle, wool. I think of the baby doll Molly loved in the toy shop, the fontanelle so realistic I could almost see it pulsing.

I could have spent this afternoon with her. She could be here, now. There's no deadline to meet; the article was written and emailed days ago, after two long sessions sitting up until midnight, drinking coffee and developing a pain in my left shoulder. I have another bag to pack, I think, smoothing Rapunzel's beaten-up head. I have a bag to pack for a small private clinic. I will pack loose cotton clothing, extra-large sanitary pads, a wash-bag, a novel I've been meaning to read for months. I will pack these things and when the time comes they will, apparently, give me thick woollen socks to wear, to stop my legs shaking, and I will lie down in a white room while a drip is slid into my arm and then they will prise me open with their cold metal and scoop me clean of a life I can't carry. A farewell-fuck baby; the night David came to collect the last of his things and I opened a bottle of Sauvignon Blanc. And then another one.

We'd sneaked into Molly's room to watch her sleeping, her tangled hair on her pillow case, her breathing. We pressed against each other, knotted our fingers. And then we stood outside the door, kissing, seeking out each other's tongues with a hunger I hadn't realised still existed. 'I'm just relieved you didn't smash the bottle in my face,' he said. And I said, 'I might, yet.'

What is it about these vicious little exchanges that stirs the blood, that twists something in the belly? A kiss that turned into an undressing, there, in the hallway – and suddenly I was on my knees, his cock in my mouth, my jaw aching, trying not to cry and wanting very much to bite.

I could pretend it was for old time's sake, for the joy of having made this perfect girl together. It wasn't. It can't be explained. Sex with the Ex. It makes no sense. It's something the body screams for when it's been hurt, a sense of completion. Look, aren't we civilised, we've made sensible arrangements for our daughter and we're parting on good terms – a farewell fuck, where he lays me down on the landing, where I reach up and pull his hair, as though I'm pulling him out by the root. And forget about my cap, shrivelling and hardening in its box. I'm spatchcocked like some hapless, drunken teenager, thinking how horrified my mother would be if she knew. A blur, then waking up with a banging head and the dried-on smear on my inner thigh. Explain that.

And a few weeks later, mixing warm milk into my daughter's Weetabix, I gag and run to the bathroom and lean over the toilet bowl. And within days my breasts feel more tender, as though they've been punched.

Tomorrow, I think, as I kneel on my bedroom floor stuffing my bag with the matronly cotton nightie I wore after having Molly, I will have the results of that foolishness, that embarrassing lapse of judgement, suctioned out of me. I tuck Rapunzel inside, next to the wash-bag with its pristine cake of unperfumed soap and new toothbrush.

I will take Molly back to the shop, buy her that doll, a doll she will love with the passionate, unconditional love we all crave. It doesn't matter about going back on my word. I hardly qualify as a responsible adult, after all. I'm a stupid girl, a girl who'd spread her legs for the man who's leaving her because she can't help herself. Because sex hurts and heals.

Let her have her doll, her baby. I'll keep Rapunzel in my drawer; poor homemade, unravelling Rapunzel. I'll remember the feeling of joy as my Granny handed her to me. 'Look', she said, 'look who I've made for you!'

I brush my hair, find ear-rings, blow my nose. Outside the light is starting to fade. I will smile brightly when I see David, hand over Molly and her bag and her dolls cheerfully. What I've made – what we've made – can be un-made. And when I wake up afterwards there won't be anything left to reproach myself with. The evidence of that night, which will look nothing like a child, will have been sluiced into a bucket, will be gone.

David doesn't know, and he won't ever find out. It's my grubby little secret; mine alone. In a few years' time he might make babies with Tashina, olive-skinned, thick-haired babies, and Molly might spend weekends with new siblings who tug her hair and chew her toys.

And me, I'll be sore for a few days and lie awake at night wishing the past had been different. And then I'll get better. I'll carry on with my busy productive life, because there is no choice. It's better to keep busy, to look at what you've spent the afternoon making, or writing, or sewing, to value who you are and what you've done. To say, look, I made that. Just look at what *I've* done.

HOUSE HUNTING

This is perfect, even better than expected. White walls studded with driftwood-framed mirrors; white-painted floorboards; a free-standing tub with clawed feet; pine shelves groaning with homeopathy and aromatherapy products; a huge, luxuriant fern glistening in a galvanised-metal bucket. And spotless. Gleaming enamel sink, chrome fish-shaped soapdish, shining Victorian-style taps. Children's bath toys stacked neatly in a stencilled wooden box at the foot of the bath (yes, I looked).

I lock the door and listen for voices. I can hear Veronica and the owner ('call me Maddy') clattering off along the stripped-pine landing. Maddy is a veteran of this game. The housing market is slow. She is forever filling the coffee machine, digging out the Hob-Nobs, whizzing round at the last minute with the Dyson. Her smile is so practised it's almost genuine, bless her. And here I am, in her bathroom, my fingers caressing the soap, drinking in the smell of clean skin.

Veronica is my latest find. The man at Handley's was showing distinct signs of fatigue, and besides he had offended me by sending grainy particulars of an ex-council house on the borders of a rough estate. I could picture it clearly: swirly nylon carpets and a muddy, sloping garden dotted with crippled and abused tricycles. Veronica is altogether more satisfactory. She has a pink calf-leather Filofax and wears little fitted jackets in pastel shades with rows of shiny buttons. As soon as I walked into the office, I knew she would be suitable.

'What sort of price range are we talking here?' she asked brightly, running the tip of her biro along very white teeth.

I mentioned a sum recently paid for a five-bedroomed, three-bathroomed villa near the park, and then began the usual speech.

'Price isn't really the issue,' I told her, tucking my feet under my chair. 'My husband's been left a considerable legacy by his aunt. He's her sole heir, you see. She was a wealthy woman – she owned a large property in the New Town area of Edinburgh. Five bedrooms, plus a granny flat. All original features. Obviously, there's a modest pension for the housekeeper, and some charitable bequests, but after that...' I spread my fingers wide. Veronica's eyes brightened and she flicked a discreet tongue over her lower lip. I leaned back in my chair and gave her my embarrassment-of-riches smile – a slight shrug, a flutter of the eyelashes.

'After that,' I continued, 'he gets the lot.'

'And...' Veronica was virtually in love with me by this stage. 'Do you have a property to sell?'

'No.' A decisive shake of the head. 'We wanted to wait until we could buy outright. Neither a borrower nor a lender be, as Gordon says. He's old fashioned,' I added, looking her straight in the eye. 'Comes from a very old and proud family.' I left out the bit about their being minor Scottish aristocracy. I had decided, after careful consideration, that this was over-egging the pudding. I felt sure it had been part of my downfall with several of the others, including the man at Handley's.

'Let me get you a coffee,' said Veronica, smiling at me as she stood up, a conspiratorial, 'at last a punter who knows a decent property when they see one' smile. She lifted the filter-coffee jug and I was pleased to see I warranted a china cup, not a chipped mug or – abject humiliation – Styrofoam.

'Milk? Sugar?' she purred.

They are downstairs now, doubtless discussing what a nice woman I am and how impressed I seem with the marble fireplaces, the plaster cornices, the original tiled hall. Oh, but I am impressed, Veronica: it's all just right. This bathroom, for example, could have been made for me. There are no fiddly cabinets to prise open – everything is out on display. His razor, her hair putty, little grey and red tubs of remedies – arnica, chamomilla, sulphur, nux vomica, belladonna; this family is all present and correct on the remedies front. Brown bottles of essential oils – rose, ylang-ylang, eucalyptus, mandarin, bergamot, grapefruit, lavender. An oil-burner and a neat stack of night lights; I run my fingertips over their waxy surfaces.

I close my eyes and imagine Maddy and her perfect husband together in a deep, scented bath. Candles lit on shelves, children homeopathically sleeping, a portable music centre playing – what? I stand with a phial of lavender oil pressed to my left nostril, concentrating. What would they be listening to in their fragrant, post-coital bliss? Vivaldi? Mozart? It will come to me later. I replace the lavender oil and unscrew the top of the vanilla-scented foaming-bath essence to dip in a finger. It tastes good enough to drink, sweet and soapy on the tongue.

This is our third property in two days. Veronica has arranged a packed schedule as I've told her I'm only here for a week, staying with an old friend. She calls my mobile to arrange appointments; she really is a credit to her profession – patient, enthusiastic without being pushy, never wasting my time with rubbish. The first house had sea views and more panelling than you could shake a stick at. Still, as I pointed out to Veronica in her car on the way back to Johnson and Cullen's, the garden was too small to accommodate a conservatory and there was slight evidence of rising damp in the downstairs cloakroom.

'Goodness me,' said Veronica, her voice slightly brittle. 'You're quite an expert, Mrs MacDonald. I shall have to watch myself.'

'Please, call me Lydia,' I said. 'And I do want to thank you, Veronica, for your patience and understanding. It's just that it's so important to me to find the perfect house and garden. We'd like...' – I gave a modest little cough, gently tapping the glove compartment – 'we'd like to start a family soon. We always said we'd wait until we were financially secure and suddenly we feel it's becoming more urgent. I'm thirty-five next month...'

That did the trick.

'Don't worry,' she smiled, pulling into the traffic. 'We'll soon have you sorted. I know you'll love this next one. Four beds, two receptions, kitchen-diner, laid to lawn front and back. Lovely neighbourhood.'

'Wooden floors?' I asked her, leaning back and closing my eyes.

'Absolutely,' Veronica assured me. 'Stripped and polished.'

Even the toilet in Maddy's bathroom is beautiful. I lift the lid and stroke its polished wood. Maddy has been thorough in her preparations for me; environmentally friendly loo cleaner rings the rim. I smile as I picture her, enthroned. It's such a great leveller, a toilet. However beautiful, however successful, however happily married, everybody has a bladder and bowels.

I put down the lid. I will give myself another minute, fingering the ylang-ylang and the eucalyptus. They smell unbearably beautiful; it's difficult to choose which to have. I decide on the eucalyptus; its sharp scent in my nostril makes my eyes open wide. It fits neatly into my bag.

The second house Veronica showed me was a double-fronted Victorian detached in the most select of neighbourhoods. I wanted to hug her; this meant I was a serious contender, in her eyes, for membership of the Des Res club. She hovered tactfully in doorways as I ran my fingertips over tiled hearths, lifted Persian rugs, blew dust off the tops of heaped paperbacks.

'Books tell you so much about people, don't they?' Veronica chattered pleasantly as we moved through the dark-red reception rooms. Obviously a literary couple, they even had a pile in the bathroom: travel books about Marrakech and Malaysia filled with photographs of viciously bright flowers; battered novels by Auberon Waugh; stacks of *Poetry Review*; large and shiny volumes about transforming your kitchen and distressing your paintwork. Most of them were too bulky to be secreted in my bag, but I found a slim volume – *Selected Poems* by T.S. Eliot – and it fitted perfectly.

'Veronica, I know you're going to be furious with me,' I said as we drove back through the leafy streets, 'but that bathroom was just too small and poky, and Gordon and I are particularly keen to have a nice bathroom.'

I'll have to go down now. The amount of time a potential purchaser can spend in a bathroom is limited. There's an etiquette to these things, and it's vital to get it right. Five minutes is acceptable, providing you've made it clear you intend to 'borrow the loo'. If only.

I unlock the door, and suddenly it comes to me: Puccini. Maddy and the perfect husband, whom I shall call Mike, would listen to Puccini, particularly the *Madame Butterfly* aria. And possibly *Tosca*. He would slide his tongue along her soapy neck, down one of her breasts, glistening like firm crème caramel, and she would taste of vanilla...

'Are you all right up there, Lydia?' calls Veronica.

'I'm absolutely fine,' I call back, looking over my shoulder for a final glimpse. I want to hold on to the memory, perfect in every detail. I snap quickly with my phone's camera; not great quality, but still.

Down in the kitchen, which is vast and painted a soothing cream, Maddy asks me if I need a second look at anything. I tell her I've seen all I need to see. I love this bit: the owner and agent smiling wide bright smiles, not entirely sure what I mean. Have I bitten the cherry? Is this delightful family home – four bedrooms, two receptions, big garden, designer kitchen, separate utility room – the one for me? Am I to be Maddy's saviour (she wants to move to a converted barn in the Gloucester countryside) and will I secure a nice fat wad of commission for Johnson and Cullen's?

'It's absolutely perfect,' I tell them both, my hand on the back of one of Maddy's beech chairs. 'I love it. I'll arrange for Gordon to come down and see it as soon as possible. I'll get back to you tomorrow at the latest, Veronica.'

Maddy cannot help herself. She throws her arms round my neck and hugs me. I give her my pleased, slightly embarrassed, really-there's-no-need laugh. I drink in the smell of her lovely blonde hair and smooth skin; she smells of vanilla.

Veronica offers me a lift back to my friend's; it's the least she can do, under the circumstances. I have to decline her kind offer, because unfortunately for Veronica, the circumstances are not quite as she imagines. My last view of her, as she adjusts her sunglasses and gives the dashboard a triumphant punch, makes my heart lurch. I am not unfeeling: I know she will be hurt and angry when I fail to phone her in the morning, and when her increasingly frantic calls are not returned.

I wait until she is fully out of view, then take a last look at Maddy's house. The daffodils in the front garden are just bursting into exuberant yellow and gold. Being Maddy, she hasn't planted them in stiff, regimented rows, but has allowed them to spring up in the lawn, in the borders, under trees. I'm sure I can hear her singing a Puccini aria from the kitchen.

I walk to the end of the street, turn on to the main road and catch a bus. The flat where Gordon and I live is the upper part of an Edwardian terraced house. From the outside, it looks reasonably respectable in a depressed sort of way. There are no rusting cars on the front lawn, but no clumps of daffodils either. The paint is peeling from the woodwork and the windows are grimy from the constant traffic. I pass through the shared hallway, with its orange and brown wallpaper, and open our front door.

Gordon isn't back from the pub yet, so I'm free to pull out the box from under the bed. I wrap the bottle of eucalyptus oil in a tissue and put it with the rest of the things, then I file the details of Maddy's house with the others and look through the Yellow Pages for more agents. I must give it a month before I try another one.

I know I'll be safe; Gordon doesn't look under the bed. He is not an inquisitive man. He used to be a sales manager with an electronics company until the firm went bankrupt and he was made redundant. At first he'd sit hunched over the newspaper, drawing rings around jobs aimed at twenty-four-year-old graduates, but he doesn't do that anymore. This year he refused to celebrate his fortieth birthday, or mine. I don't nag; I'm the only person he has, really, except his Aunt Peggy. She still lives on the council estate where she brought him up and she sends him a cheque from her pension from time to time.

As for me, I haven't worked for a year, since they caught me stealing from the petty cash in the property company in Clapham where I was an accounts assistant. Personnel agreed not to prosecute, but they never mentioned a reference, and I didn't feel I could ask. They couldn't quite look me in the eye when I collected my coat.

I get undressed in the bathroom. It has what is called a 'coloured bathroom suite'. The colour is dirty plum. The carpet, which stinks of urine and damp, is chocolate brown. I used to scrub the bathroom every day when we first moved here, but it didn't make much difference. The mould grows freely around the toilet and sink, like eruptions of eczema on skin. You can scrub it off, but it always comes back. We had a nice bathroom in our old house, our real house, the one we had to give up when we couldn't pay the mortgage: a white bathroom suite, sleek chrome taps, white tiles. Not as perfect as Maddy's, not as classy, but not like this.

I run the hot tap and pour in some Tesco Family Bubble Bath, which makes me want to laugh and cry at the same time, because there will be no family. I'm sorry, Veronica, I really am. Babies aren't an option when your man's got no sperm.

I close my eyes and imagine I'm Maddy. I'm lying in the swirling bubbles, scented with vanilla, and I'm sipping a gin and tonic with lots of ice. The kids are downstairs in the sitting room, watching a Disney DVD, the big one cuddling the little one; there's a macaroni cheese in the oven and a salad with Lollo Rosso, avocado and a scattering of pine nuts in the fridge.

I hear Mike's key in the lock. I smile to myself. When he comes in, I lift my long, slippery arms out to him and tell him I've got a lovely surprise, that I want to see his face when I tell him the good news about the charming cash buyer who was particularly impressed with the bathroom. He whoops with joy, and starts to undress. He can't take his eyes off my breasts.

THE CASTLE

Ella decides that today she will build the entire town, large and complicated with winding streets running down to the sea, and a marketplace where women with red-checked headscarves and fat brown arms sell bulbous tomatoes the size of apples. She'll start with the castle for the king, queen and princess. The sun punches her neck and shoulders as she shovels sand into the larger of the new buckets, bought for her yesterday at the beach shop. It is good sand here, firm and dark and slightly damp, with bits of crushed-up diamond that sparkle in the sun; she pats it down hard and smoothes the surface with her spade, ready to turn it upside down and make the main hall of the castle.

Further up the beach her parents lie on identical sunloungers, reading. Their skins shine with suntan oil; they are darker than at home, like over-ripe plums, and she cannot see their eyes, hidden behind the dark blank rectangles of sunglasses. Her father is reading *The Times* and frowning; her mother is leafing through a fat, shiny magazine, occasionally drawing hard on her cigarette. The smell of the smoke catches on the breeze and drifts towards Ella. Even before the holiday, her mother has been smoking a lot, leaving ashtrays dotted around the house, on the edge of the bath or by the telephone, so that the whole place seems to shift under an uneasy aura of tobacco. Now she is flicking ash into a little polystyrene cup, half buried in the sand; her fingernails are sharp and red.

The queen, Ella decides, will not smoke. She heaps fresh sand into her bucket and adds another wing to the castle. The queen will sleep with lavender under her pillow and will smell of new bread and freshly ironed cotton. The queen will not ignore the princess when the princess brings her drawings to inspect or cardigans to unbutton. Ella sits back on her heels to admire her handiwork and plans the queen's bedroom. She will have her own turret, giving her a commanding view of the landscape, and her dresses will be made of devore and lace and her pillows will smell of jasmine and vanilla. She will wake fragrant and smiling, stretching long, pale limbs, and the princess will snuggle into bed beside her on warm mornings and together they will enjoy the feeling of warm skin and quiet breathing.

The queen and the princess will not behave like Ella's own family in the mornings, Ella decides. In Ella's house, her mother gets up in a rush, her breath smelling of Marlboro Lights, and bangs around the kitchen barking instructions and telling Ella to *get a move on, child.* The au pair, Heidi, who is in love with a boy called Gerald and spends a lot of time weeping or painting her toenails, drives Ella to school, while Ella's mother goes to work in an office where she writes advertisements for lipstick or chocolates. Ella's father leaves for work so early that she hardly ever has time to say goodbye; sometimes she catches the sound of his sports car roaring off into the distance and hears her mother muttering at the slammed door.

Ella begins to dig the moat around the castle, to keep the bad people out. The princess can decide when to let down the drawbridge and trip daintily across on her favourite conker-brown horse, its hooves skittering on the hard surface. Ella digs the moat good and deep, scooping spare sand away with her hands. She looks back at her parents; her father has put down his newspaper and is watching her and smoking a small, strong-smelling cigar. Normally he only smokes cigars after dinner, when he goes sits on a chair on the patio, one side of his face lit by the security light, staring out across the lawn, rubbing his toe against the leg of his chair.

Her mother stubs out her cigarette in the polystyrene cup, which fizzles and starts to disintegrate.

'Go and get her an ice-cream, or something,' she says. 'It's the least you can do.'

'She's busy,' says her father. Ella wishes she could see his eyes behind their dark glasses. It's as though they might not be there any more.

'Oh, well then,' says her mother, laughing in the way that means something isn't funny, 'don't bother. Don't stir yourself.'

The king in Ella's castle will have a kind face. He will not wear sunglasses. His eyes will be on show; he will look straight at people, and they will know what he is thinking. His breath will smell of peppermint. Ella pats down the sides of the moat so they are smooth and firm, and brushes sand from her palms on to her swimming costume.

'How's it going?' asks her father, leaning forward. The dark skin of his belly is stretched taut above his swimming trunks. The skin is so tight, it look almost as though it might split. He is hairy as a wolf, dark springy hair erupting on his chest and belly and legs. The king will be smooth all over, like a fish.

'I'm doing the moat,' says Ella. She stands up, goes down to the water's edge and scoops up a bucketful of sandy water. Further out, the sea is kingfisher blue, almost painfully blue to look at, dotted with swimmers and small boats. Parents shriek to their children in French: their voices sound louder and shriller across the water. Ella's mother can speak French; in the hotel, she speaks rapidly, rolling her eyes, using her hands, touching her shoulders. Her father says nothing.

'They love it when you make the effort,' Ella's mother says, turning away from him at the breakfast table, pouring strong bitter-smelling black coffee. Her father sips his orange juice in silence.

Ella's bucket is full to the brim; she staggers as she carries it back to the castle; the weight of it makes her shoulders ache and her knees buckle.

'*Help* her then, for God's sake!' snaps Ella's mother, as her father half-stands, one knee resting on the sunlounger. 'Can't you see she's struggling?'

Ella's father squats down beside her on the sand; his breath smells of cigar smoke and sweat glistens on his face.

'May I be your assistant?' he asks her.

She can see the beach and the castle in miniature reflected in the dark mirrors of his glasses. She sees herself, squatting, staring at him. She looks tiny, like a squashed-up doll.

'You can do the houses,' she tells him, 'for the servants. With the small bucket.'

He works quickly, breathing hard, filling the bucket with sand and turning out houses with swift, compact movements, arranging them in rows, as Ella instructs. She gathers tiny pink and cream shells and works on the decorations for the castle, studding the walls with slivers of shell. The tide is coming in. Families pick up their deckchairs and towels and retreat up the beach, nearer to Ella and her parents. Ella notices her mother frowning as they approach; her lips tighten and she lights another cigarette, props herself up on one elbow and leans forward.

'You might as well tell her now,' she says, speaking louder than she normally does in public. Ella's father flinches. He seems mesmerised by the sand houses, smoothing their edges, running his thumb around the tops, pressing his knuckles into the sides to make windows.

'I thought at lunch,' he says, and Ella's mother snorts, hard.

'Ella,' she says loudly. 'Daddy has something to tell you. Something he's only recently told me and something he should have told us all a long time ago. The trouble with Daddy is, he's a coward. He does despicable things and then he's too spineless to...'

Ella sees the French families staring at her mother. She hunches over the princess's turret and presses in more shells. She's aware of her father and mother standing, facing each other, shouting and snarling; she's aware of the hot sun burning her neck and the suck and hiss of the sea as it ripples across the sand and then retreats. She presses her face down next to the castle; sand sticks to her cheek. She imagines the king, the queen and the princess, holding each other's fingertips and dancing, a slow, circular dance. She squeezes her eyes shut and stuffs her fingers in her ears. If she concentrates really hard she knows the sounds of the sea and her parents' voices will disappear, and all she will hear will be melodic, resonant laughter from inside the castle.

THOMAS

He's a gift, wrapped up in a blue fleece snowsuit, his cheeks flushed pink in the cold air. Six months, possibly seven, Ruth guesses. He's slumped asleep in his buggy, left negligently outside a crowded shop in The Lanes, the kind that sells hippie nonsense – perfumed candles, joss sticks and dream-catchers. His stupid mother is presumably inside, buying things she doesn't need. Dangerous things, things a baby could choke on, or reach out for and burn himself. She crouches next to him, drinks him in. His mouth puckers on a dreamed teat, and his breath, his breath – that shockingly familiar scent of apple and milk. His top lip is slightly chapped. He needs her.

The blood roars in Ruth's chest.

Her hands grip the handles and in seconds she's kicked the brake, lowered her head and is pushing him into Brighton's shopping crowds. And away. She walks quickly, not quite running, steering deftly, avoiding ankles and dogs. A plastic Tesco bag, full of that woman's junk – a glossy magazine, two nappies, a half-eaten cheese-and-tomato sandwich in plastic packaging – bangs against her knees. She stuffs it into the bin by Pizza Hut. *We won't need that, Thomas, we have everything we need at home. Much nicer things.*

He sleeps on as she crosses Western Road, despite the buses, the cars, the noise. So many people: the January sales and all everyone seems to want is more stuff, more furniture for their houses, more clothes for their backs. Look at them all, hefting their Debenhams and M&S carriers, none of them taking any notice of their tired, fractious children...

He's such a good baby. At the traffic lights she squats down just to watch him breathe.

'Sweetheart,' she whispers as they cross the Level, 'stay asleep now. Just until we get in. Everything's waiting. Everything's just the same.'

There's a sharp, blue edge to the air as she pushes the buggy – oh, the beautiful weight of him! – past the hulking teenage boys zooming up on their skateboards in their ridiculous baggy jeans and backwards baseball caps. Bad skin, bad language, the grind of wheels on the pavement. Too close. She grips the handles tighter, keeps her head down. She's forgotten the ache of the shoulders, pushing this weight; how every muscle strains to hang on, to keep him safe. The boys shout out to each other and she wants to gag them. *Don't you wake him,* she thinks. *Don't you wake my baby.*

No one familiar at the crossing as the green man beeps; head down, up Southover Street. This part of town's so steep, like plodding up a mountain; she'd been back in her jeans three weeks after giving birth. Her breath comes in little dragon puffs and her lungs feel ready to burst. Her heart bangs in her ears. So wonderful to feel this hammering, this *lub-dub, lub-dub.* For the last six weeks, since that awful night, she's wondered if it still works or if her body's running on autopilot because her heart has died. David says not to think like that, but he hasn't been ripped apart like she has...

Another five minutes and we'll be safe, my darling baby. We'll be safe inside.

A car backfires and he starts, his eyelids fluttering for a moment, then he sinks back into sleep.

Nearly home, Thomas, we're nearly home now.

At the corner of Grove Street she pauses for a moment, panting slightly; important not to rush. Not to run. Running with a buggy is irresponsible, dangerous. She used to have nightmares about her hands slipping on the handles and the buggy careering down the hill to crash into an oncoming car, her precious boy smashed...

Don't worry, Thomas, I won't let go.

'Hello, Ruth. Oh...'

Maggie, from over the road, with her brick-red wind-chapped face and bright yellow fleece. Whose fingers were always dirt-stained after afternoons on her allotment; who'd come round, the day afterwards, with a bunch of papery white roses she'd grown herself, weeping and not knowing what to say. Like all of them. The house had been full of flowers for weeks, like living in a florists, drooping, blousy blooms everywhere.

Go away, Ruth thinks. *Just piss off.* But she forces a smile.

'Hi, Maggie. A lovely day. Are you off to dig?'

'Yes,' says Maggie, but Ruth knows she's not concentrating; she's looking down at the sleeping baby, as though she can't believe what she's seeing, as though she can't believe his beauty.

'Well, enjoy yourself,' says Ruth brightly. 'Don't get cold.'

'No,' says Maggie, fiddling with her zip. As Ruth smiles and walks on, she hears Maggie call out, 'Ruth, are you...?'

'I'm fine. We're all fine.'

Walk quickly, but don't run. She'll be gone in a minute and we'll be inside. Once we're inside no one can stare or ask questions. We'll be safe then.

Here's the house, darling. We made it.

She wants to laugh for pure joy.

She flips the brake and digs in her bag for her keys. He's still asleep, bless him; he's always been a good sleeper. He doesn't even stir as she pushes the door open and gently tilts the buggy backwards to lift the front wheels over the threshold.

She's forgotten how much of the tiny hallway the buggy takes up. She holds her breath, squeezes past and pulls off her gloves. She hangs up her coat, scarf and bag and listens to the sound of his breathing. He's staring to stir; little grunting sounds.

The silence in the house has been one of the worst things, like a toothache that won't shift. She'd tried to block it out, leaving the radio on as she cleaned every inch apart from his room, but it was there all along. The absence of him.

She kneels down next to him as his eyelids flutter open. His face is even more beautiful than she'd first thought, flushed after that brisk walk through the cold air. His pale, gingery eyelashes are long enough to brush his cheeks. His mouth opens, closes, opens; goldfish lips. She loves the faint, tremulous quiver of his nostrils.

'We're safe now,' she whispers, and suddenly a muscle jerks under his left eye and his eyelids bat and flutter and he's awake.

His eyes are blue-grey, like the sea on a winter's day. Exactly as they should be. Perfect. He takes a few moments to yawn and focus, then turns his head towards her and stares directly into her eyes.

He recognises me, she thinks. *He knows who I am.*

He's perfectly still. Silent. He doesn't take his eyes from her face, reading her hairline, eyes, nose, lips, chin.

'Oh, clever boy. My clever, clever baby.'

She unclips the straps, gathers him into her arms and the weight of him... *This*, she thinks, *is what no one understands.* How when your baby's gone what you miss is that backache, that weight, that soreness in the arms and shoulders. When the paramedics tried to take Thomas away, she'd held on so tightly it took two of them to prise her fingers from his shoulders and legs. She'd felt her wrists would crack with the force of their grip.

She carries him into the living room and cradles him on the sofa. He fidgets and squirms but doesn't cry out; he's still watching her, intently. She lies him on his back and eases off his pale blue hat. Strawberry-blonde hair pings from the static, like thistledown or a dandelion clock. He has perfect little rose-petal ears, with plump lobes.

Like Thomas's. She'd always been amazed at the perfection of his ears.

'You're beautiful,' Ruth tells him, leaning close and smiling, and he reaches up and grabs her mouth, pulls at her lower lip. His fingers are cold and taste of saliva. She kisses them, one by one, then pulls down the zip on his snowsuit, frees his arms and then his legs, bending them carefully at the elbows and knees. So easy to accidentally hurt a baby when you're undressing them; they're still fragile, however robust they appear. She tugs the snowsuit off. Underneath he's wearing a blue and green striped sweatshirt and miniature baggy jeans. She doesn't like them; the denim's too stiff for a baby's delicate skin. And pale blue socks, faded from too much washing. Maybe he's wearing hand-me-downs from older brothers; no doubt that woman's got several kids. She leans into him again and he tugs at her hair, grunting with satisfaction. She loves the tugging at the roots and squeals with mock-pain; he looks into her eyes and grins. She can see the white stubs of two tiny teeth breaking through the perfect pink gum.

'Come on, my darling,' she says, kissing his bright cheeks, his vanilla-scented hair. 'Let's get you into your proper clothes.'

His room smells a little musty and feels cold. She opens the clown-patterned curtains, raises the blackout blind and the two of them blink in the sudden light. David and her mother cleared up after

Thomas was taken away; she couldn't come in here at first. Everything is just as it was, she wouldn't let them change anything: the big pine cot with the pale blue cellular blankets, the clown mobile he'd loved and gurgled at first thing in the morning – how she'd loved that sound, crackling through the baby monitor by her bed – the changing table, its wipes and baby lotion neatly lined up. The wind-up cars in the toy box that made him screech with delight and flap his arms as they scuttled across the floorboards. The white-painted chest of drawers, with all his clothes, neatly folded. All the new ones friends and family had given her for his next growth spurt; everyone said how much they grew in that first year, almost overnight...

She lies him on the changing mat and smiles into his eyes as she eases the button and fly of his jeans. She peels them down, loving his chunky, pistoning legs, the dimpled knees. Once they're off she drops them into the bin. She pulls off the sweatshirt, too, and bins that. She doesn't want him wearing old stuff. Not now he's hers. Everything he has from now on will be just for him. She undoes the poppers of his vest and slides it over his head; she can't stop herself from kissing his warm, pulsing belly, his chest with the heartbeat dancing underneath. His skin smells biscuity, delicious. He gurgles and kicks with both feet and reaches out for her hair again.

She takes off his nappy, heavy and sodden, and cleans gently between his legs, telling him how good he is. His penis is a perky little shrimp and his testicles are floppy and relaxed. His skin is slightly red where the ruff of the nappy has chaffed against his thighs. She rubs in zinc and castor-oil cream. *That's better, isn't it, Thomas?* He's good as gold as she takes his ankles in her hands, lifts his bottom to secure the new nappy. He wants to be here, with her. Everyone knows babies won't let you change them without a fuss if they don't trust you.

'Nice and dry now.' She settles him on her hip as she rifles, one-handed, through the drawers to find better clothes. A pure cotton T-shirt and Gap tracksuit bottoms. The dark blue jumper her mother had knitted for him for when he got to this age...

Downstairs the telephone starts to ring. She ignores it. Getting him dressed is vital; he needs to be warm, comfortable, and now she's dressing him *properly*, as her *own* baby. She finds some clown socks and hands him one to chew as she pulls the other one over his perfect, straight toes.

The phone carries on ringing. Usually people give up after nine or ten rings – she used to count, for the first few weeks after it happened – but this goes on and on.

She carries him downstairs, her perfect boy, and picks up the receiver.

'Ruth.' David's voice is low and calm. She likes his calmness; he's never been one to shout. He's usually measured, rational. 'How are you doing, love?'

'I'm fine,' she tells him, and then covers Thomas's cheeks with delicate butterfly kisses. 'Went into town. Very crowded. Had a coffee at Costas. I was going to get myself a new coat in the sales but I couldn't see anything I liked.'

Thomas grunts and tries to grab the receiver, curling his fingers over her hand. Ruth laughs; he's so bright, her baby, so spirited.

'Ruth, what's going on?' David sounds less calm now; she can hear the tension rising, like when he tells her she should go and talk to someone, keep seeing that idiot counsellor or try to go back to work or do anything that takes her away from the house and what happened.

'Ruth,' he says again. 'I've just had a call from Maggie and she says you've got a baby.'

She can hear his panic, his fear. She hates that; this is no time to shout. Shouting and tension are bad for babies. After they'd taken Thomas, after they confirmed he was dead and they were very sorry and they would let them have some time for themselves before the doctor came and they sat on those horrible purple sofas in the relatives' room and he tried to hold her and his face was all red and blotchy, she'd shouted, screamed at him that they were lying, that she would never let her baby...

Now she nuzzles her chin over the baby's hair.

'It's wonderful, isn't it? He's fine, he's beautiful. Totally healthy. I told you. And you wouldn't listen and I'm right. I've been right all along.'

'Ruth, tell me what's going on – what are you doing? Ruth, what have you done?'

'I've got him back,' she says calmly. 'And everything's fine, David, everything's absolutely fine. Trust me.'

She replaces the receiver. She'll have to act fast, this time, before they take him again.

Nearly lunchtime; more people on the street. Jim from next door going for his pint at the Albion, a few mums beginning their treck up the hill to Queen's Park to collect their little ones from nursery. She's aware that people are staring and she ignores them. The air has warmed up and the frost on the cars and rooftops has melted. It's a perfect day, luminous and clear, and she knows exactly what to do. She's full of an energy she thought she'd never feel again, and Thomas is happily kicking his feet and drinking from the Tommee Tippee cup – he likes his milk warm, and she's packed some rusks for later.

Down the narrow side streets to the sea. The crowded pavements, so difficult with a buggy; crossing by the Sea Life Centre, wait for the green man, wait, wait, don't rush. Cross again and there's the pier, the scent of chips and hot dogs and candyfloss and doughnuts and the distant throb of music. Down the ramp to the beach, past all the shops selling postcards and buckets and spades and body boards. *Look, Thomas, look! The beach! We're here!*

He'd always loved the beach, the shushing of the waves and the foam bubbling and sparkling across the shingle. Ruth hums and pushes faster along the walkway, then squats down, snaps open the straps and lifts him out. Seagulls scream overhead and there's a sharp, salty breeze in her face. The sea is beautiful today, so green and restless. She hugs him tight, rubs her cheek against his cold, pink face as she carries him – slowly, carefully – across the stones.

FRIDAYS

'Oblige me with the usual, Julia, there's a dear,' says Theo. I slide out of my clothes and into the severe black uniform he has thoughtfully ironed, aired and hung on the back of the bedroom door.

I lace my voice with as much venom as I can muster; authentic detail is important, as Theo frequently reminds me.

'Take *that*, and *that*, you disgusting creature!' I yell at him as he cowers and sobs. 'Perhaps *this* will teach you not to read that vile and poisonous filth! Hail Mary, Mother of God, hail Mary, Mother of God, this is for your own good, you wicked, debased creature. Hail Mary, Mother of God...'

He is a big man, tall and well covered, and his belly hangs in folds. When he cries his eyes become bloodshot and his nose runs. Naked he looks all of his seventy-six years, with liver spots on his hands and a dewlapped chin.

'That was marvellous,' he says afterwards as I rub in the baby lotion. 'Do you know, when I close my eyes, I could swear Mrs Douglas is in the room. You capture her tone perfectly.'

We watch the lunchtime news and eat spaghetti bolognese with long silver forks. Theo is a wonderful cook; he adds fresh basil to the sauce and sprinkles flat-leaf parsley over the pasta. Everything is served on the best china and the wine is pleasantly robust. Theo likes to get the details right; it vexes him if his sauce isn't perfect or his salad icily crisp.

He promised from the outset that he would always provide the meals for *our little arrangement.* We met a year ago at the local drama group during a production of Ionesco's *The Lesson.* I hadn't done any acting since I was a child; I'd grown shy and self-effacing after years at home with the kids. He played the professor; a teenage girl with alarmingly mobile features was the young girl; I played the housekeeper. Theo always made a point of praising my performance. After rehearsals he walked me to my car, telling me I had a serenity that shone through on stage. He was magnificent as the professor – subtly menacing, pressing the tips of his fingers together as he spoke.

After the final performance he threw a party in his glorious Georgian flat in Sussex Square. The drawing room was papered in dark-red paper with gilded cherubs. My husband, Paul, sniggered at how camp it was; we live in a modern house, open plan, with white walls that show every mark and watercolour prints from a shop on the High Street.

Theo served ice-cold champagne and fragments of smoked salmon on minuscule squares of toast, difficult to hold. He waited until Paul had been cornered by Irene Lucas, the director, before guiding me to a sofa.

'What extraordinarily pretty fingers you have,' he said, taking my hand in his. 'Delicate, but strong. A good grip. They remind me very much of our housekeeper, when I was a child. She had care of me in the school holidays.' He gently squeezed each of my fingers. 'She was a very religious woman,' he added.

After lunch I order him to lie face down and tie him up with thick brown stockings – American Tan, eighty denier. I tell him he's a worm, a slug, not fit to slither across the earth. He doesn't mind me reading his *Hello!* magazines while I abuse him. I have to keep an eye on the clock, though, so I can get changed in plenty of time to pick the children up from school.

'Mrs Douglas, have mercy,' he whimpers. 'Surely I am not so totally worthless and revolting...'

'You know you are, you vile abhorrence of nature,' I snap, interested to discover that Liz Hurley and I have similar taste in cushion covers. I've always yearned for strong colours, reds and golds and purples; Paul thinks they're vulgar and dated so all our cushions are cream. 'You'll stay like that until you realise the full extent of your depravity. Stop wriggling, or I'll fetch the carpet beater.'

'These knots are hurting my wrists,' he moans. 'I'll tell my mother.'

I throw down my magazine, kneel on the carpet and put my face next to his, sneering just the way he likes it.

'Your mother is a whore,' I whisper into his face. 'She couldn't care less what happens to you. She's down at the docks, opening her legs for sailors.'

'No, no, she's a lady, she gives tea parties, she wears silk dresses!' sobs Theo. 'Oh Mrs Douglas, why are you so cruel?'

'Because it's fun,' I spit at him. I check my watch. 'Sorry, Theo, I must dash. I was a bit late last week and Lucy was upset.'

'Of course, my dear,' he says, lying quite still so I can wrestle with the knots around his wrists and ankles. 'You really did excel yourself today.'

The money is in a pink scented envelope, as always. Theo gives me the left-over bolognese sauce in a Tupperware container; he says it's too much for one. He takes my hand and kisses my knuckles. He helps me on with my jacket. Outside the air has turned cold; I hurry across the park, hugging my arms around my body, aware that he's watching from his window.

'Did you have a good day?' asks Paul over dinner. He commutes into London and always arrives home hungry.

'Very good, thanks,' I tell him. 'Met an old friend for lunch.'

'I'm glad you're getting out more,' says Paul. 'You seem a lot happier. You've got quite a spring in your step these days.'

He nuzzles my neck as I load the dishwasher. The children are in bed; I know he'll want to take me upstairs.

'That was a marvellous meal,' he says, leading me out of the kitchen. 'The sauce was perfect.'

'Let me help you with that,' says Theo as I struggle to cover the backs of my shoulders with cocoa butter. 'Goodness, we're nearly out of this stuff. I'll have to get some more.'

'It's probably cheaper to buy it in bulk,' I tell him, securing my white lace cap with kirby grips. 'Try Superdrug. They've got some really good special offers at the moment.'

'Thank you, my dear, I will,' he says. 'Are you ready?'

'Yes, absolutely,' I say. 'Get on the floor, you little scraping of excrement. Start licking.'

Theo has thoughtfully placed a folded towel on the piano stool so it's not too cold when I sit down. I'm pleased my rendition of 'Ave Maria' runs more smoothly these days; when we first started my playing was embarrassingly rusty. I learned piano at school but I gave it up when I started working so by the time I'd married Paul and had the kids I'd lost the confidence to tackle even the basic pieces. Of course we don't have a piano at home – Paul says it would look out of place. So I practise secretly on my son's keyboard after Paul has left for work and by now I can thump out the required tunes with some degree of confidence.

Theo positions himself by my toes and darts a nervous tongue over my ankles.

'Harder, harder, you vile little pervert,' I yell. 'Don't stop until

I give you permission.'

The rendition takes less than five minutes, by which time he has nearly reached my knees. I used to worry the cocoa butter would make him feel sick but he insisted that to him the taste was heavenly. I switch to 'In the Bleak Midwinter'.

'Please let me stop now, Mrs Douglas,' he pleads.

I put my foot on his head, and press.

'Not until I say,' I sneer. 'Not until you've learned your lesson.'

'I hope the heating was on high enough today,' he says afterwards. 'This flat can be so draughty in winter.'

'It was absolutely fine,' I assure him. 'Theo, that looks delicious.'

'Cock-a-leekie,' he says proudly, spooning the soup between my lips. 'I made it last night. There's a bread-and-butter pudding in the oven too.'

'My favourite,' I tell him. 'You do spoil me.'

'Nothing's too good for you, Mrs Douglas,' he says, and his eyes fill with sudden tears. He rests his hand against my cheek. His fingers are cold and stiff, with ridged, horny nails.

'She taught me to cook,' he tells me. 'She was wasted as a housekeeper. She had enormous talent, wonderful flair. Even during the war she made the most delicious dishes – sorrel and nettle soup, lava bread, honey-roast chicken. She was terribly resourceful. She killed the chickens herself; I used to stand by the back door watching her through my fingers. She had beautiful hands, a pianist's hands, but strong, deceptively strong. Her wrists were like iron.'

After he's cleared the plates away I lock him in a cupboard and shout things about his mother through the keyhole. I tell him she's a tart, unfit to breathe the same air as the God-fearing. As his sobs reach a climax I inform him that she's gone away, perhaps for good, that she's left me in charge and that his father's dead. When he's really wailing I go back to the piano and bash out 'Mine Eyes Have Seen the Glory of the Coming of the Lord'.

'I've put a little extra in this week,' Theo tells me, handing me my scarf. 'You really are growing into the role.'

'See you next Friday,' I tell him. He stands at the window and waves. From the park he looks old and tired, chilly in his burgundy dressing-gown.

During the week I go to the supermarket, vacuum the house, volunteer to decorate the school hall for the forthcoming nativity play. I fill the manger with straw and paint gold stars on a navy backcloth. The tinsel halos look lopsided; my hands tremble as I shape them. The other mothers chat and laugh and agree they all loved acting when they were children. They remember the moment the lights picked them out on stage, the *oohs* and *aahs* from the audience. They remember hilarious scenes when baby Jesus rolled out of his crib or the Mother of God picked her nose.

My son, Miles, is the innkeeper; my daughter is an angel.

On Thursday I go shopping with my money from Theo. I buy a tight black cocktail dress and black silk underwear from a boutique in Hove. When I look at my reflection in the changing-room mirror I seem thinner; my eyes are huge, my face harder. Theo is right about black: it makes any woman beautiful.

In the shoe shop I try on black stilettos. I wobble at first; I've never had heels that high. The sales assistant smiles knowingly as I hand her my credit card. On the way home it feels cold enough to snow.

'You've missed a bit, you defective little slug,' I tell Theo as he crouches by the skirting boards with his J-cloth. He's wearing pink Marigolds and a submissive expression; goose pimples have appeared on his arms.

'Sorry, Mrs Douglas,' he whispers. 'I'll try harder.'

'Get on with it and shut up,' I snap, opening a fresh *Hello!* and flicking ash on the carpet. 'You are not here to speak, only to serve.'

After he's finished I tell him to sit cross-legged on the floor and polish the silver. He winds the cloth between each fork-prong, frowning with concentration.

'Will my mother ever come back for me?' he ventures timidly.

I throw the magazine at him.

'Of course not. Why should she?' I laugh. 'You're a worthless piece of scum. You desire the other boys. You watch them. It's all round the school. She's ashamed of you. All you're fit for is mindless servitude.'

'How cruel you can be, Mrs Douglas,' he whimpers. Droplets hang from his nose and he brushes them away with his forearm. 'Shall I put these away now?'

'Yes, hurry up,' I say. 'Then start on the bathroom. I want to be able to see my face in those taps.'

Theo makes ricotta and spinach gratin for lunch. He likes us to feed each other; it's fiddly but we manage without too much mess. A few shards of spinach end up on my uniform. He lights church candles and puts on a CD of Gregorian chants. The nuns' voices, painfully pure, fill the room.

'She used to take me to Mass on Sundays,' says Theo dreamily as we lie on the sofa, his head on my breast. 'Ten o'clock. The church was as cold as death. It seemed as tall as the sky and I thought God was sitting in the rafters, looking down at me. They had enormous candles, the colour of bleached bone. She made me kneel on the floor; she thought cushions were sinful. The altar boys used to swing the incense around and it got in my eyes, my throat. You could smell God in that place.'

Outside, on the way home, the light is sharp and clear and the freezing air hits me in the teeth.

'Is that new?' Paul asks as he hangs up his suit. 'It's brilliant. Have you been squandering the child benefit on cocktail dresses?'

'I got it in a sale. Fantastic value.' The lie slips out easily; sometimes it excites me to deceive him. 'Shall I try it on?'

He moves his fingers up my leg.

'I bought new shoes, too. New spiky shoes. Very strict.'

Afterwards there's a small creamy stain on the fabric. Paul is asleep within minutes.

I know there's something wrong the moment Theo opens the door. He's dressed to go out, in a thick tweed coat, deer-stalker and scarf.

'I was waiting for you,' he says. 'I didn't just want to ring your mobile – I don't like to leave messages. I wanted to speak to you...'

'Theo, what's the matter?' I ask. I've never seen him so agitated. His eyes are swollen and his hands are trembling.

'Your money,' says Theo, handing me a pink envelope. 'There's extra, too, for the inconvenience. I may be a while – they couldn't say exactly how long it would take...'

'What will take?' I ask. It's icy in the flat and dark; he has drawn all the curtains. There is a faint, lingering smell of wax.

'It's her,' he tells me, fiddling with the strap on his suitcase. 'Mrs Douglas. They've moved her to a hospice near Bournemouth. She retired down there. I'm getting the train. A taxi's coming at eleven.' He starts to sniff. 'Oh, Julia. It's cancer, everywhere. They rang me last night.'

I try to picture Mrs Douglas, small and stiff with pain.

'She loved me, you see,' says Theo, taking my hands. 'She was the only one. She didn't have to stay on but she did. She was only hard on me because she cared.'

He drops my hands and lights a cigarette with shaking fingers.

'What about when you get back?' I ask. My voice sounds thin and lost in the dark room. 'Will you still want me to come?'

'Of course,' he says, not meeting my eyes. 'Of course I will. You're wonderful. You have always understood.'

I kiss his cheek. 'Take care, Theo.'

'I'm all she's got,' says Theo. 'I'm not much, but I'm all she's got.'

He watches me from the window as I cross the park and we wave to each other. My throat aches. A taxi arrives and he climbs in slowly, wrapping his coat around him like a shroud. I watch the tail lights disappear around the corner, the exhaust fumes lingering like smoke from an extinguished candle.

Back home I sit at the table, smoking and fingering the pink envelope. I will leave it a week before I ring. Theo will be upset but he'll need me more than ever. When she's dead he'll crave to be reminded of her even more: her hands, her clothes, the way she made him pray.

Perhaps I'll leave it for two weeks. Or perhaps he'll call me first. He might even need me before next Friday.

I go upstairs, change into my tight black dress and watch my face grow sharper in the mirror.

SOW

Bless me, Father, I have sinned. Really *badly* sinned. And it's been... I guess it's twenty years since my last confession. I thought I'd have forgotten what to do, but it all comes back to you, doesn't it?

Father, I'm here because twenty years ago – Bella, she was called. It wasn't just me, Father, and it wasn't my idea but...

I wish I could say that when I first saw her I really liked her, or I could see how pretty she was, or I saw past all the... *fat*, Father, but that would be a lie. That would just be the things you're meant to say to make yourself sound less shallow, and I'm not here to lie. And I didn't mean to stare, because Mum had told me not to, because Bella was a 'poor soul' who deserved compassion and couldn't help the way she was. But Dad, even though he never met her, said she'd be a great blubbery useless sow, that people who were that fat were just lazy and greedy. So that first time...

She lived in a ground-floor flat in a block on one of those rough estates; she'd been there about five years, Mum said, and she'd never been out. Mum was a carer for Social Services, Father, she had a key and let us in. The hallway was painted a horrible dark pink – I remember that – and the carpet was an orange swirly pattern. Mum called, *Yoo-hoo, Bella! It's Maureen, love!*

We went into her bedroom and it was very warm. The whole place was warm, I think the heating was on, even though it was summer. And the bedroom was all pink, too, but a nicer pink, Barbie-doll pink, and everything very frilly and girly – flowery pink curtains and a matching bedspread and little pictures of dogs praying. It smelled of roses – and I liked that. And she had this big dressing table with a portable telly on top and lots of little china animals and a silver photo-frame with a little girl's face in it. And in the corner was this huge commode with a towel over it.

And then this massive bed – the biggest bed I'd ever seen, Father, bigger than a normal double bed. I think you'd call it *empire* size. And in the bed – propped up on lots of pink pillows, and taking up most of it – was Bella.

She was gigantic – not just fat. I'd seen lots of fat people before – my Nan wasn't exactly skinny and most of the women in our street, by the time they'd had a few kids, were big. But she was just... Father, she was so big that her head seemed too small for the rest of her, it looked all wrong, if you see what I mean. She had these... eyes that were buried so deep in her face you could hardly see them, and her cheeks sort of... flapped, and her nose was squashed looking. Her skin was red and greasy, like she'd been working really hard and got all sweaty. And she had a little round mouth – I remember thinking it looked like the sort of mouth that was always sucking a lollypop – and then under that she had layer after layer of chins... rows of them. And she had whiskers, too – dark curly whiskers, some on her face and some on her chins. It was weird, Father, to see all that fat on just one person; I remember thinking, are there really two of her? And she had dark frizzy hair sort of *sprouting* on to the pillow – and these huge shoulders. And she was wearing a lemon-coloured nylon nightie, like an old woman, but she wasn't that old, she was way younger than Mum. And then her arms... very white, they were, lardy, like they'd never seen any sun... great *wobbling* flesh hanging off them. And her breathing was very loud and slow, like she'd just run upstairs or something, like she was... panting... with effort. I think it hurt her, Father, just to breathe.

And the oddest thing, Father, were her hands. She had these weird little hands – like a child's hands... they didn't seem any bigger than mine – just loads fleshier. And her fingernails, I noticed her fingernails – they were so pathetic, Father, because some had bright pink nail polish on but mostly it was chipped off. I remember thinking that was really sad.

And Mum said, *Bella, love. I hope you don't mind but I've had to bring my little girl with me today. She's called Amy. She's no trouble, she'll just sit nice and quiet and do her drawing and what-not in your front room...*

And Bella said, *Oh, the little duck! Oh, she's a sweetheart.* Her voice was deep... growly... like a big man; like my Dad's. And she kind of panted when she talked, and licked her top lip afterwards. And then she said, *Come here, my lady, let's have a proper look at you.* I glanced over at Mum and she nodded and I went and stood by Bella and we locked eyes. She reached out with her little fat hand and stroked my hair.

Oh Maureen, she said to Mum, *she's lovely, she's a pet. She's a princess.*

And Mum said, *Well, she's not too bad.* She was trying not to smile even though I knew she wanted to really. We didn't go in for a lot of praising in our family, on the grounds it wasn't good for you. I'm the youngest of seven, Father. *She's quiet anyway*, Mum said, and suddenly, I don't know why, Father, but I just blurted out, *I could paint your nails for you, Bella.*

Mum tutted, but Bella... Oh you know when people say 'her face lit up' and you think, yeah, but it didn't really – well hers really did, her skin was really glowing. And she said, *Oh, would you, pet? I'd love that! Would you really do that for me?*

Mum said, *I'm not sure about that, Bella, she might make a mess, she's only ten.* But I said, *No I won't, I've done our Diane's loads of times.* And Bella went, *I've got some polish, duck, in the top drawer – oh please let her, Maureen.*

So Mum said yes but it had to be later, after she'd made Bella all nice and comfortable. She shooed me out of the bedroom while she gave Bella her bed bath – because there's no way she'd have got her into the real bath. And I heard them both grunting as she helped Bella to sit on the commode, and then Mum flushing the toilet afterwards, and I didn't want to think about that, Father, because it all seemed so intrusive – like being a toddler, having to be put on the toilet... I mean, she was so enormous I guess she couldn't even wipe herself, and that's horrible, isn't it, like you've got no dignity left? And I sat in her front room, which was all tatty with just a gas fire and some saggy old furniture, and I drew Bella as a princess. I gave her a long pink dress and made her hair long and curly and made her much slimmer. And I drew her standing up, with her arms outstretched and her fingers pointed.

And that was how it started, Father. While Mum was hoovering the rest of the flat, and making Bella a cup of tea, I got all the stuff out of the drawer. She had a perfect manicure set... and I sat on the bed and spread a little towel under her left hand first and rubbed Astral handcream all over the skin, like our Diane had taught me. Our Diane was training to be a beautician and that's what you do – you prepare the whole hand so the client is nice and relaxed. And I massaged her palms and wrists and she loved that; I don't think anyone had held her hand for years, Father, isn't that sad? Isn't that just the saddest thought – that no one had held her hand or stroked her fingers?

I did a really good job on those nails. I took off the old varnish with remover and pushed back the cuticles, gently because they were all ragged – she liked that – and I filed the nails down a bit and made them a nice crescent shape. And then I painted them pink for her, dead carefully, like a real manicurist would. And we talked about how we both liked to draw – she wasn't right keen on reading, she liked her telly better, but when she was a little girl she used to draw all the time.

When I'd finished painting her nails I lifted her fingers to my lips and blew on the varnish, like our Diane did with her own nails. You weren't supposed to do that with clients, but I knew Bella wouldn't mind. And when it was all finished Bella had tears in her eyes. She said, *No one's ever given me a manicure before, pet. This is the happiest day I've had for years.*

Then she hugged me and I felt myself... disappear into all those soft rolls of flesh and it was like I was suffocating, like all my breath had been taken away.

And then she said, *I feel like you're my best friend, Amy. I wonder if you'd do me a little favour? Would you, lovie, would you be really kind and do me a favour?*

I pulled myself away. I was feeling a bit sick actually, and I asked her, *What?*

And she said she had a bit of a sweet tooth, and the people who brought her meals in, they were very mean about it. And she liked a little bit of chocolate now and then when she was watching telly of an evening. If she gave me the money, could I get her some, bring it with me next time?

I asked her what she wanted and she said, *Mars Bars, Maltesers, Topics, Milky Ways,* and then she told me where her money was and it was in the drawer of her dressing table. So she said to take a tenner and get as many as I could and hide them in my rucksack and not to tell anyone, and I could get myself a Mars Bar too, for my kindness. And I folded the money up and said I would. And she scooped me up for an even closer hug and I could smell her – she didn't smell nasty or anything, she smelled of soap, but I hated all that flesh, Father.

Mum came in then and Bella held up her nails to show her and Mum started smiling and shaking her head and saying I was a right little madam, but actually, Father, I knew she was proud of me, because I was being kind. She was a kind person and she thought that to be Christian, really Christian, you should be kind. You should show your kindness in deeds, not just thoughts and words.

And after that, all through the summer holidays, I went to Bella's with Mum twice a week. She had other people coming in and doing things for her, but she liked us best. Actually, she loved us. She loved Mum because everyone loved Mum – she was saintly, everyone said so. And she loved me because every time I went, after Mum had helped her on to the commode and washed her and all that, I emptied out all the chocolate bars and bags I'd bought and she hid them under her pillow and said I was an angel and her best friend.

And then I'd massage her hands and paint her nails. I took some of our Diane's old polishes with me – pinks and reds, yellows and oranges, even greens and blues – and sometimes I painted a rainbow on Bella's nails and she'd laugh and say, *Look at me, I'm fit for a night out with a handsome fella, aren't I?* And I combed her hair for her sometimes, she loved that. She found it difficult to reach because her arms were so fat. And I started taking old blushers and eye-shadows round and making her face pretty and then showing her in the mirror. I suppose she must have looked ridiculous, more like a clown than a lady, but she didn't mind. I think, Father, she was delighted. If you could have seen her face, the way she glowed, you'd not have thought badly of me.

Not then.

One day I asked her about the little girl in the photo and her eyes got all glassy and tears ran down her cheeks and I had to dab them away because they made the blusher all streaky. She said, *That's my own little angel. My Kelly-Marie. She's sixteen now. They promised me they'd bring her to see me every week but she hasn't been for four years.* And she snivelled and I had to give her a tissue to blow her nose, a right big bellowing blow it was, Father, and she said, *They poisoned her mind against me, that's what they did.*

I combed her hair and pulled it into a sort of bun and showed her how she looked. She liked that. *That's classy, that is,* she said and she was still sniffing and laughing and crying all at the same time. She didn't mind how sad she seemed. It was like I was the powerful one, Father.

Then one time Stacey from next door came round. She was rough, was Stacey, she could do the most horrible Chinese burns if you didn't do what she said. I didn't usually play with her – Stacey went to a special school because she'd been kicked out of ours. I told her I couldn't play with her because I was going to work with Mum.

And Stacey laughed and said, *But she's a bum-wiper, isn't she? What do you do, wipe bums with her? Ugh, that's sick. You're weird, Amy Allen.*

And I shouldn't have... but I... I told Stacey about Bella. And once I'd started I couldn't stop myself. I told her how huge she was and I enjoyed watching her eyes go wide and glittery when I said how Bella took up the whole bed. How she was like a giant woman. I said, *You know what I do? I paint her nails and do her make-up and she says I'm the only person in the world who's ever done that for her. And she gets all soft and soppy and goes on about her girl, who got taken into care. And she's all sweaty and she wears these horrible old nighties like she's your Nan or something...*

Oh, Father. I'm sorry, I promised myself I wouldn't cry... I expect you're thinking what a right horrible brat. And now I'm sorry for myself and that's pathetic. It's Bella I should be sorry for. I'd like to say it was because I was so scared of Stacey, that if I didn't come up with a good story she'd give me a Chinese burn or pull my hair. But you know what? I was sick of Bella. Sick of all that flesh.

The size of her. She was so... soft. Sometimes I thought she had no bones underneath all that fat – that she was like a big squashy cushion, and if you jumped on her really hard nothing would crack because she was all fat and nothing else. And while Stacey was standing there I remembered what Dad had called her and I just blurted out, *She's like a pig. Like a – like a sow!*

And Stacey said, *Bloody hell. A sow. Right. So where does she live?*

I went cold then. Stacey was dead hard and a gang leader. So I said I couldn't remember and then Stacey pushed me up against the wall with one hand and grabbed my ear with the other and said, *Think on, Amy Allen. You've been there often enough.*

So I told her the address and she said, *Right. Let's pay her a visit. Let's tell her what she is, the great fat sow!*

I thought I was going to wet myself, I was so scared. I said, *I can't, Stacey, I won't be allowed*, and she hissed into my face, *Be round here at nine o'clock sharp or I'll knock your teeth out.*

That night Mum and Dad went out to the Social Club and our Diane and her boyfriend were meant to be looking after me but actually they were in her room with the door locked. So I sneaked round to Stacey's, wearing a big dark jumper and a woolly hat, because Stacey said. I was sweating, Father, it was August, still warm. It was a bit drizzly and I remember how uncomfortable I felt in all those clothes. And there were all the kids I was never allowed to play with – Dean Jackson and Simon Bailey and the Whittaker twins – and we got the bus over to Bella's estate.

When we got there it was still quite light so we hid in the bushes under her bedroom window for a bit – but we couldn't really see anything because she had the curtains drawn so she could watch her telly. We could hear a bit of the noise from the programme and then the ads – *Melts in your mouth but not in your hand.*

I imagined her lying there, eating the Maltesers I'd bought her, and doing her slow breathing.

And then Stacey pulled out a pot of black paint and some brushes from her bag – and she took off the lid and we all dipped our brushes in and wrote horrible things on the wall under her window. Stacey wrote GREEDY BITCH LIVES HERE and the Whitaker twins wrote FREAK LIVES HERE although I don't think they spelt FREAK right, actually, and Dean wrote the F word because I think that was the only thing he could write and Simon painted a – well, it was a male organ, Father, sorry – and I... I wrote FAT SOW. And then Stacey took the brushes back and put the lid on the paint and I thought that was it. I was feeling frightened, Father, but also... pleased; like I'd finally said it, the thing I wasn't allowed to say about Bella.

So I whispered to Stacey, *OK so we're going now?* And she just looked at me like I was something she'd trodden in, and then she took a brick out of her bag. Like a normal house-brick. And she held it up and whispered to the rest of us, *When I chuck this, everyone shout summat and then we're off. Right?* And we all nodded.

Stacey pulled herself out from under the bush and then she threw the brick and there was this huge crash and Bella's window splintered and there was glass all over the place. And then we all just screamed out – *fat bitch, fat bitch, you greedy effing monster* – things like that –

And Bella, screaming. *Oh, oh, oh, go away, go away!*

And then we all legged it down the road and someone opened a door and there was a man's voice shouting *Oi! You little bleeders, I can see you, get out of it right now!* And I'd be lying if I said it wasn't exciting, Father, the adrenalin pumping as we ran and hid in a back alley to get our breath back. And then when we'd stopped laughing and saying how great that was, we sort of dawdled back to the main road, pretending to be great mates. And the bus took ages coming and we'd stopped talking to each other by then and by the time I got home I just felt sick. And dirty. I remember washing my hands so much they went red and raw and thinking I'd never get the black paint off. And that night I couldn't sleep, just lay and looked at the ceiling and car lights sweeping across it and wondering how Bella was. If someone went to help her. If she was still crying.

The next morning when I came down for breakfast Mum and Dad were sat at the kitchen table and Mum was looking really sad – she'd been crying, her eyes were all pink and she kept blowing her nose. She said, *I've had a phone call from work, I've got some bad news, love. Some horrible hooligans went round to Bella's flat last night and smashed her windows and yelled nasty things at her and she's had a heart attack. Like your Granddad. She's in hospital and she's unconscious...*

I went cold all over. I said, *Is she going to be all right?* And Mum said, I don't know, love. *I don't think so, no. She's very poorly, you see. I want to go and see her but they said only relatives.* Mum blew her nose and hugged me. *Oh, poor Bella, poor love!*

And Dad tutted and said, *Some kids today, I tell you what, love, they've no respect. They all want a bloody good hiding. Any kid of mine that was disrespectful to a disabled person...*

And Mum snapped, *Well, you're a fine one to talk. You were quick enough to pass judgement, call her names! She's a lovely lady, for all she's so large. She's gentle and kind and our Amy was very fond of her. Weren't you, love?*

And I nodded but I'd gone dumb. All weak at the knees, Father, I had to sit down. My stomach was full of butterflies. I thought I might pass out. I almost wished my dad *would* give me a hiding, just get it over with. The worst thing was, he saw me looking all sad and he scooped me up and sat me on his lap and put his arms round me because by this time I was crying, that snotty sort of crying where your whole face just leaks. He hardly ever showed

any affection, Father. So this was like the worst punishment ever –
because by rights I should have been feeling the back of his hand.
Not his sympathy.

And Mum lit another cig and smiled at him sadly and said,
You're just as soft as our Amy, you, when it comes down to it. And he said,
*I don't like to see my special little lass upset. At least we know we brought
our kids up right.*

Bella never came back from hospital. She never regained conscious-
ness and they couldn't save her. They said it was her weight – *mor-
bidly obese*, it said in the paper. Mum was allowed to go and see her
in the end, she was in intensive care, all wired up to machines.

And that night I had a horrible nightmare and I was must
have been calling stuff out because when I woke up Mum was sitting on my bed and looking at me, very hard and straight, and she
said, *Amy. Do you know something? Do you know who did that to Bella?*
I got hysterical and I was sobbing *No, I don't know anything, no, no,*
and Dad rushed in and told her to stop talking about that woman
because hadn't she caused enough trouble? And Mum gave me a
hanky and tucked me in and they left me. I could hear them rowing
about it downstairs for ages afterwards.

No one ever caught us, Father, any of us. No one could iden-
tify us because we weren't local and anyway I'm not sure any of Bella's neighbours really cared that much. As though we'd said what
they were all thinking and saying behind her back.

And after she died, Father, soon after that... everything I put
into my mouth felt disgusting. Gross. Like ash. Or slime. I'd always
been quite small and skinny but then I got... ill. I'm still really thin,
actually. People think when they see me from behind that I'm a kid;
when I turn round and they see my face I can see them thinking,
wow, it's a woman.

People are weird with you when you're very thin. They

feel sorry for you but you're also a threat. It's like you're spoiling the party, I guess. It's like they're a bit disgusted by you; like your organs are too near the surface of your skin; like your veins all show through. I do work, but I never got very far. I didn't do that well at school; I was in and out of hospital, you see, *worrying everyone sick*, as my dad said. Sometimes, even when I was wired up to drips and that, he used to look at me like he hated me. Like I'd let him down by trying to disappear.

I went back and saw Mum three weeks ago, Father. She was in a hospice and then two days later she died and then we had the funeral. And when we had our last conversation, even though she was off her head on painkillers, she said to me, out of the blue, when I was holding her hand, *Remember Bella? You used to paint her nails, love?* And then she opened her eyes really wide and looked straight at me and said, *What really happened, Amy?* And I pretended I hadn't heard and started talking about our Diane's kids and she closed her eyes and pulled her hand away.

Thank you, Father. I will say those prayers – every one of them – and I will think of you. And yes, I hope for peace in my heart again one day. I might come back – if that's all right. I'd forgotten how soothing it is, to confess. Like feeling God sat next to you. Like He's listening to you and you actually matter. Like He's stroking your hand when no one else in the world wants to touch you.

THE ASCENSION OF MARY

Mary Heap first realised she could fly while queuing for cheese at the delicatessen counter at Sainsbury's. She was standing behind a fat man in a raincoat when suddenly her feet tingled and she found herself floating several inches above the floor. Now she was level with the top of the man's head and could see the oily tram-lined hair against the pink skin. She felt queasy at the sight of so much scalp at close quarters and returned to the ground. But she was too excited to wait to buy Eric's cheese, and left.

All the way home on the bus, she remembered the sublime sensation of floating. She tried a little levitation, just enough to put a distance between herself and the seat. She had a better view from this position: the cars and people in the street shrank, squat and foreshortened, beneath her gaze. She descended gently with a delightful bump. She felt light as air as the bus pulled in to her stop.

In her kitchen she practised rising and falling slowly, to the shipping forecast. It was a question of establishing a rhythm, she realised: not too much thrust on the uplift; hold the legs steady; don't forget to use both arms. She thought of squally seas, light-houses lashed by gales, and imagined herself hovering above rocks, flicked by an occasional burst of spray. She put a Taste the Difference lamb casserole into the oven and then rose above the lino, critically examining the tops of the cupboards. By the time Eric came home she felt she was getting to grips with floating, bending her knees for take-off and landing, moving her weight on to the balls of her feet. It was a struggle to remain seated as she faced her husband across the table.

'Any cheese?' asked Eric, wiping his mouth. He liked a bit of mature cheddar with oatcakes and pickle. He said it gave him strength for his swim. He spent several evenings a week at the local pool, thrashing the water with his pale arms. Swimming dried out his skin, leaving it flaked and raw in places, and a faint suggestion of chlorine hung about him for hours afterwards.

'Sorry, love,' said Mary, piling dishes. 'I forgot. Something came up.'

Next day Mary practised her flying. After Eric left for work she drew the curtains in the front room, closed her eyes and allowed her body to rise up, up, until her hair brushed the ceiling. She lay flat and paddled her limbs, discovering she could fly out to the hall and up to the top landing. It was while she was improving her technique that she thought about flying outside, soaring through the sky with the birds, looking down on towns and villages, seeing lakes reduced to puddles and fields to little green squares. She'd always wanted to go in an aeroplane but Eric said the very thought of it made him feel sick.

On Thursday evening she microwaved a chicken fricassée and watched Eric chewing, twenty-four times a mouthful. She finished her own meal quickly and stood behind him. He had thinning grey hair, swept sideways to cover the bald patch. He had little bodily hair left; his skin was as smooth and cold as a fish. Mary put out her hand and touched his neck, tentatively. He stiffened.

'I'm thinking of getting a bus tomorrow,' she said, 'out to Ilkley.'

He stopped chewing. 'Whatever for?'

'Oh, I don't know,' she said, gathering plates. 'Just to have a look around. I haven't been anywhere for ages.'

After lunch next day Mary put on two jumpers, folded a fleece under her arm and boarded a bus for Ilkley. She sat on the top deck, right at the front, unable to resist the occasional secret lift, to get herself in the mood. It was the end of September, still sunny but with the first nip of cold puncturing the air. The light on the hills was clear and sharp; the views would be wonderful.

At Ilkley she headed towards the moor, greeted two Americans with rucksacks, and then found herself alone. She struggled into her fleece, feeling suddenly self-conscious, like a badly wrapped parcel. Her heart pounded in her chest. Was she fit enough for this? Would her muscles cope with the strain of the extra distance? Then she looked up at the clouds, bent her knees, pushed her feet against the ground and rose, her skin tingling at the sharp rush of air past her face. She moved her arms and legs, cautiously at first, then more confidently, delighted that flying was so much easier outside, so much more natural with no ceilings to impede her progress, no danger of bumping her head against the pendant lights. This was how birds must feel – limitless space, sky that went on for ever and ever. She laughed out loud.

As she climbed the air punched her teeth, making them ache. Mary sailed over the moor, south towards Bradford. She and Eric had always lived in Bradford. When they first married, thirty years ago, there had been talk of moving out to one of the nearby towns or villages – Ilkley, Otley, or maybe even Keighley – when the babies arrived or Eric got the better job. But the babies never had arrived and Eric never had got a better job, and he decided not to bother with a car, with everything they needed being so local, and he continued working for the council. So they had stayed, and Mary stopped looking at baby clothes in catalogues and at photographs of cottages in estate agents' windows. She was made redundant when they privatised the school-meals service – she was only fifty-four and so she thought she might as well take on some voluntary stints at the Help the Aged shop. Soon she found herself identifying with her elderly customers, feeling greyer and more faded month by month. She hung bags of nuts out for the birds and watched them cling on with their wizened, old-man legs and then soar off into the sky. Sometimes her heart lurched, watching them.

Mary looked down on Saltaire, Salts Mill huge against the neat rows of houses and gardens with billowing washing, and then flew on to Shipley, where she found herself directly over a primary school. In the playground girls were French skipping and boys were playing football; from above they looked like fast-moving navy-blue insects. She wondered if any of them would glance up and notice her. None did.

'I've not seen you here before,' a voice shouted behind her. Mary almost lost her balance and found herself flapping wildly, craning her neck to see who had spoken. A woman of about her own age, wrapped in a lurid purple tracksuit and blue fleece, swooped up behind her.

'I'm Pam,' said the woman. 'Pleased to meet you.'

'I'm Mary,' said Mary, feeling her cheeks burn. She always found introductions difficult. 'It's chilly up here, isn't it?'

'Oh, you need to wrap up,' said Pam cheerfully. 'You'll have to invest in a nice tracksuit – more practical than elegant – if you're going to get serious about this. And thermals. Worth every penny when there's a nip in the air.'

'Thank you,' said Mary awkwardly. 'Yes, thank you, I will.'

'If you don't mind me mentioning it,' said Pam as they dropped down over Manningham, the Bradford City football ground deserted and Lister's Mill glinting in the thin sunlight, 'your technique's a bit patchy. You want to hold your shoulders steady and regulate your breathing. Saves energy. Have you been flying long?'

'No, not long,' said Mary, beginning to laugh. 'I thought it was just me.'

'For Heaven's sake,' said Pam. 'What an idea! Here, Sue! Sue!'

Another woman, squeezed into a pink velour outfit topped with a bobble hat, flew up alongside.

'You'll never guess,' said Pam to Sue, 'Mary here thought she was a one and only.'

'Oh, I've been at it for years,' said Sue. 'Thursday's my day normally, but then they changed the rosters at work. There's nothing like it for the circulation.'

'My husband says that about swimming,' said Mary.

'Not the same thing at all,' said Sue. 'You have to look up all the time, if you don't want to drown.'

'Quite right,' said Pam. 'Water's not the place for human beings. You can't breathe properly. It's not natural.'

They flew over the city centre where women struggling with toddlers and buggies shopped singly or in groups. Mary thought how tired they must be, how worn down by their lives, while she and Pam and Sue soared effortlessly over the Wool Exchange and then headed towards the Law Courts. Below them traffic jostled bad-temperedly and a van screeched to a halt at a pedestrian crossing. Mary stretched her arms out wide, tingling to the tips of her fingers.

'Coming in for tea?' Pam asked. 'We normally stop for a cup about now, don't we, Sue?'

'Oh, you have to give yourself a break,' said Sue, 'or you really feel it in the shoulders the next day.'

'Just off Great Horton Road,' said Pam. 'Number fifteen. Mind out for that chimney.'

They hovered above the rooftops, catching their breath. The sun had almost disappeared and Mary felt suddenly thirsty and tired.

'You can always pop in if you're in the area,' said Pam. 'Land in the yard if you're coming from above. Only mind the bins, they can be treacherous.'

'That's a lesson I'll never forget,' agreed Sue. 'It certainly pays to plan your descent.'

'Thank you,' said Mary shyly.

Inside Pam's kitchen Mary peeled off her fleece and one of her jumpers and enjoyed sweet tea and Jaffa cakes. Pam and Sue offered to call for her the next time she fancied a trip.

'Do you normally start from home, then?' asked Mary. She could not imagine launching herself from her back yard, in full view of the neighbours. 'Doesn't anybody notice?'

'Nobody notices middle-aged women,' said Pam, wiping crumbs from her mouth and stretching her legs.

'She's right,' said Sue. 'There's lots of us at it. You don't need it when you're younger. You're looking upwards anyway. You think you can fly without even trying.'

'But after you hit fifty,' said Pam, 'then it really is your time. Anyone want another Jaffa?'

Back home Mary unpeeled the frozen lasagne and remembered the green moors sprawled beneath her, the grey city with its ponderous buildings and sudden emerald parks, the ant-sized people swarming across the pavements. Her hands seemed heavy and huge as she struggled with the packaging; she remembered how light they had felt in flight, slipping through the air like feathers.

Eric was home at six thirty sharp, as always, and tea was ready at six forty-five. He read his paper. Mary toyed with the salt cellar.

'I went up there today,' she said.

'Up where?' he asked, scratching his neck.

'Ilkley. It was lovely. You can see for miles.'

'Oh aye. Any more of that sauce?'

It was stuffy in the kitchen; steam misted over the panes. Mary opened a window, glad of the cold air on her face and neck. She breathed more easily.

'You can't see out in this place,' she said, scraping more pasta on to his plate. 'We should go up there. You can get a bus.'

'Be easier with a car,' he said. 'Buses take too long.'

Mary's fists tightened. 'We haven't got a car.'

'There you are, then.'

'Eric,' she said, 'I can do something, something really wonderful.'

'Oh aye. What's that then?'

He continued to chew. She remembered her first sight of him, in the cinema queue. She had seen him from behind and felt sorry for him because he was hardly taller than she was, and his ears were bright red, and they stuck out. On their third date he tried to persuade her to go swimming, but she just sat on the poolside, flinching whenever she was splashed. She felt a coward, rooted to the ground, watching Eric's muscular arms thrash through the water. She thought he'd be a good hugger, passionate and strong, with arms like that.

'It doesn't matter,' she said. She thought about the irresponsible joy of flying, the wind in her face, of looking down and laughing. 'I'll make us some decaff.'

That night, as Mary sat in front of her mirror combing her hair, she caught sight of her face, still glowing. From the bathroom she could hear Eric spitting out the mouthwash.

Eric climbed into bed and began to read the sports pages. Mary stood in the middle of the room and felt her feet prickle, the carpet rough under her bare toes. She rose very slightly in the air.

'Eric,' Mary said suddenly, 'look. Look at me. Look at me.'

She sprang into the air and flew around the room, frantic with laughter, bumping into the wardrobe, knocking a picture askew with her foot. Looking down at her husband's upturned face, she saw his pale moist eyes bulge and his mouth open and close, like a fish, drowning in air.

RECLAMATION

Suicide, sweetheart, was the easy bit.

Fifty paracetamol, bride-white and lumpy on the tongue, ten shots of Johnny Walker, Bach's *Sonata for Flute and Harpsichord in E-Flat Major* playing in the background, and the deed was done. Twilight hours of drowsing, while the music looped back on itself and the house grew colder, and then the breathing, slowing to a whisper, like a sinner in confession.

Outside, heleniums, achillea, cannas, solidago and kniphofias blazed in terracotta pots; bees, fat with pollen, lumbered through the late-afternoon heat. Frogs gleamed briefly on lily pads, then dived. I left you a wonderful garden to remember me by, my darling.

On that day you were in Birmingham, addressing a sales conference. I imagined you with a sour taste in your mouth, which you put down to the previous evening's chicken biryani, talking to rows of upturned faces about 'closure.' And there I was, 'closing', in our very own living room. I thought you might appreciate the joke, but I should have known better; irony was always lost on you, love. A gorgeous body, eyes to drown in, but a literal mind.

You found my note while the paramedics shovelled me up, zipped me into a body bag and carted me away like a sack of garden refuse. You sat on the sofa with the blinds still down and the music still on and howled, the tears and snot running into your mouth. You were a most unappealing sight, my darling. I thought you might be dignified by grief; men like you, with good skin, firm stomachs and glossy, floppy hair can look even sexier in the grip of great emotion. You went redder and redder, your neck bulged over your shirt collar, your fingers shook and you cursed me for my cowardice, for my rejection of the prospect of drugs, pain, long nights with my head over the toilet bowl watching long, opaque strands of vomit leap from my throat into the water. Or of dancing widdershins round a maypole, chanting positive messages to align myself with my spirit guide, or whatever other hippie clap-trap the 'alternative healers' advised.

What I had in mind was a quiet funeral, as I'd tried to tell you, many times, as you turned your face away and said, 'There's no need for this, babe. You're going to get better.' I wanted it to be just the two of us, intimate once more; me one side of life, you the other. Minimum number of guests; respect for who we were. No religion, white lilies only, and definitely no singing. Your response? You booked me into the local Methodist church and persuaded the wall-eyed vicar to spout a lot of nonsense about what a wonderful person I'd been. You invited the entire bloody Grief Squad. People I'd never liked warbled 'My Way', very badly, and snivelled through the whole hideous service, complete with out-of-tune organ and sprays of gaudy carnations and Marigold-glove pink roses. Bored toddlers whined and picked their noses during the final blessing.

Outside it was a gloriously hot day with bright blue skies and rushing white clouds. Inside the church it was cool, clammy, damp as fresh clay. You shivered, my love. You sent me to meet the Maker I didn't believe in, you had me burned, like one of your disastrous attempts at barbecuing steaks. You kept my charred remains on display on top of the television so the Grief Squad could admire your understated taste in urns – despite my firm and oft-repeated wish to be scattered from Mount Caburn on the first decent breeze.

Certain members of the Grief Squad – notably Sukie Chidson, the bleach-blonde bitch – even slipped upstairs to 'borrow the loo' and tiptoed into our bedroom to stare at my half of the bed. All they found were a few hairs on my pillowcase; the one you couldn't bear to change.

I was convinced you'd miss me so much, miss what we did together so desperately, that you'd join me as soon as you felt able. I had visions of you following suit with the whisky and paracetamol. You always said I was the one with the good ideas.

Do you remember how the consultant who broke the news smelt of marzipan? He avoided my eyes and shook my hand reluctantly, as though my bad luck might rub off on him. You gripped my hand while he talked at me. My hands looked much older than yours, wrinkled from sun and rain and earth, older through illness; I remember noticing just how smooth yours were, the nails cut clean across, the cuticles pushed firmly back. I brought your clenched fist to my lips and kissed your knuckles. You told me, later, you took this as a sign that I would agree to all the poisonous treatment Mr Marzipan was offering, all the chemotherapy and hair loss and non-stop nausea. You were so wrong. I simply wanted to let you know we could still fuck that night.

'Let's try all the alternative stuff, then,' you said, once I'd explained my position vis-à-vis the hospital's torture regime. 'It's got to be worth a try.'

'There's no point,' I told you. I wanted you to shut up and

lie back. You were at your most appealing silent and supine, your outrageously long lashes brushing your cheeks.

You turned away from me in bed that night, as though the slow deterioration of my flesh was already visible to you. You had no idea what it was like – you, who'd sailed through life with hardly a day's illness, who woke every morning with the blood singing in your veins. You imported the Grief Squad in droves, the faith healers, the mad Reiki specialist who claimed she'd distance-healed her brother's arthritis over the telephone to Canada, the shoulder-kneaders and soothers, the whisperers and chanters. One of them even had the nerve to tell me to 'focus on my chi' or some such crap. You watched them lay their clammy hands on me, smiling into my face. You frowned when I made them flinch. *Well*, I used to think, *positive think this*. Terminal illness is a bastard and there's no comfort in beanbags and vitamins and being massaged by a half-wit God-botherer. Or new-age guru (who used to be a wise old Indian chief in a former life, of course), invariably with enough positive energy to drown in.

Sod that.

You admitted my breath stank. Right up until the end you wanted *other* people to touch me, stroke me, press against me if necessary, but you kept your careful, hygienic distance. That's when I knew how much I revolted you. When I drank the final Johnny Walker I kissed the rim of the cold, clean glass and thought of your teeth under my tongue.

You rang your mother every night for a week. You had a fortnight's compassionate leave, and you wanted compassion.

'It was just so unlike her,' you sobbed. Your mother, who'd always hated me, snorted. 'She waited until I was away to do it. If only we'd talked, if only she'd said how she really felt...'

You rang your mother every other night in the second week.

You told her I'd been selfish, a bitch, more interested in my garden-design business than in our marriage. So untrue! And your bitterness shocked me. Your face grew leaner and harder; you hardly bothered to shave and dark shadows bloomed like bruising all over your chin and throat. Of course I'd loved my job, loved the thrill of turning a patch of scrubby lawn and a few straggling borders into a glorious green loveliness, the gritty pleasure of good true earth under my nails, the smell of my skin after a hard day's digging; but it wasn't my whole life. Our marriage was a glorious union of opposites. I was salty, woody, my fingers tasted of tobacco; you tasted mostly of indoor things – biscuits and clean linen. I liked to jump on you when you were doing your sales figures, drag you off to bed, tie you up and graze your skin with my greedy teeth, watch your eyes widen when I straddled you, brandishing the masking tape.

You must admit, love, we had our moments.

You went back to work. You stopped going to the gym, slipped into lethargy. You came home to microwave your roast beef, Yorkshire pudding and two-veg dinner-for-one and watch holiday programmes where lively families of four colonised some Croatian poolside. Some evenings you watched porn DVDs and undid your trousers and wept. You lay back on the sofa, crumbs scattered over your open shirt, slid your hands down and down and jerked with admirable energy, shouting out my name as you spurted. You never seemed satisfied. You never understood your body like I did, which delicate buttons to press, how to flutter fingers against flesh, how to massage that thin strip of skin running the length of your lovely cock. How to crack the code that led to pleasure.

Afterwards you wiped your hands on a tissue and stumbled off to the kitchen for a bottle of French lager, letting the answering machine pick up the messages from your mother and the members of the Grief Squad who hadn't had a big enough piece of your action.

(Correction: *my* action. It was my death, after all.) Then you sat back and fell asleep with your mouth open, and when you twitched awake, at 2am., you groaned, swore, limped stiffly upstairs, shuffled off your clothes and climbed into bed. You'd rarely slept naked in our last weeks together. You'd worn your pyjamas like armour, buttoned up in case I did the unthinkable and tried to make love to you. Now you rolled into my space, into the shape I'd left in the mattress, clamped a hand over your limp cock and slept a fitful sleep until 7am.

You went away to a conference in Manchester and stayed in a hotel filled with thick-waisted businessmen where you were eyed up by a woman in a red suit a size too small, her face roughened by years of late-night Chardonnay and low-tar cigarettes. The air-conditioning roared on warm evenings and vile muzak tinkled in the bar. You ate at a table for one and downed glass after glass of the house red, which stained your teeth blackcurrant-blue and left your eyes red and hooded. Although, to me, you were still gorgeous.

You told anyone who asked that you were lonely, that you felt so completely alone. The woman in the red suit sat up with you late into the night, aiming her wrinkled cleavage at you, laying her painted nails on your arm, saying she knew what it was to be lonely.

Oh my love, you were never alone. I was with you always.

In your room you drank most of the miniatures from the mini-bar, lounging on the bed in your creased suit and scratching your balls through your trousers. I was with you, my darling, sliding into the empty space to be beside you. Sometimes I think you felt me there, felt the pressure of my hand between your legs, a chill in the air you couldn't understand, my breath in your face. Sometimes you screwed up your nose and frowned, as though you could smell me still.

We could have gone on like this indefinitely, I suppose, until you'd cracked under the strain and joined me. But then the Grief Squad took you firmly in hand. And Sukie.

Our dear GP, he of the irritatingly jolly manner and execrable taste in 'comic' ties, recommended that you see more of your friends to help you 'come to terms with bereavement'. You'd turned down one-to-one counselling on the grounds that you needed to 'share' my death with others; it wasn't something you could cope with without a chorus of sympathetic clucking. You sat opposite the appalling Sukie at a dinner party organised by no-chin Jeremy, who seemed to think that having had his own 'issues with depression' before attending an 'introduction to counselling' course qualified him to gather together the saddest people he knew, serve them miniature portions of rubbery polenta, and bask in the warmth of their gratitude. To my horror your eyes devoured Sukie's tight nylon blouse, the line of sweat between her breasts, her plump, mobile thighs. She was so utterly wrong for you; I couldn't believe you would even look twice at her. Sukie, it transpired, was there to lay bare the bones of her dead mother, who, according to her sob story, had demeaned and humiliated poor Sukie and left her 'terribly insecure'.

'And now I'm free of her,' she snivelled. 'And yet I miss her, I miss her.'

I bet she didn't miss Sukie.

You sat side by side on her sagging brown sofa eating peanuts, you wallowed in her pity, you swallowed her line on karma and fate. You spent your lunch hours with her in The King's Head, drinking dry white wine while she filled herself with Bacardi and coke and crisps, listening to her little tragedies. The terrible mother was joined by a cast of other demonic characters: the distant, disciplinarian father, the bitch of a financially successful sister, the estranged brother in Australia. Her glasses misted up; dark stains bloomed in the armpits of her tight, diaphanous blouses; her neck flushed puce.

You came out stinking of salt and vinegar, holding her plump, hot hand, telling her she was a wonderful person. And then you went back to your desk and wrote her name on your jotter pad while you clinched deals and kicked ass. Your sales figures rose; your boss commented how glad he was you'd 'got over your difficulties.'

You sat in Pizza Hut – typically naff – with Sukie, strands of mozzarella spiralling down your chin, earnestly discussing how my negative energies had contributed to my cancer, with your mouths full. Then you stood on Worthing beach together, throwing stones into the ragged surf and 'saying goodbye to me'.

And then you brought her back to our house – our beautiful, understated, white-walled Victorian Brighton home with its lovingly restored fireplaces, with the houseplants I'd nurtured already wilting or dead. She sat in the perfect walled garden, murmuring how she couldn't understand my liking for 'all these dark, spiky things'. She prodded my Festuca glauca: it cut into her fingers.

Inside the house, she shivered.

'These old houses are very chilly. Must be the bare floors.'

She lay back on my half of the bed in her nasty clothes and lifted her skirts to reveal rounded mottled legs.

'I can't help feeling I'm being unfaithful,' you panted, your face in her hair, pulling at elastic, pawing at her baby-pink knickers.

'Don't think of this as infidelity,' she whispered, ripping open your shirt. 'She's gone. She's at rest now. She'd want you to be happy.'

Would she, bollocks!

I watched the two of you, snarled up in our bed, the white linen I'd chosen, her head knocking against my beautiful wrought-iron bedstead, the one that accommodated the handcuffs so obligingly. I watched the blood rush into your face, heard the yelping noises you made, the ones you used to make for me. And I burned.

Thirteen months and three days after my death, you made her your new bride.

The wedding was a riot of white nylon; Sukie looked as if she'd collided with a pair of net curtains. She insisted on church, although she didn't believe in God, because she said she liked the atmosphere, the incense, the candles. Maybe she thought the subdued lighting made her patchy complexion less obvious. (Wrong there, Sukie.) Her sister turned up wearing black and a disdainful expression. You shivered in a grey morning suit, a limp pink carnation dying in your buttonhole. Your family, whom I'd never liked, at least had the grace to look sniffy about the haste with which you'd entered into this new union.

I was with you, my love, when you took your vows. I was the rush of cool wind past your ear, the trembling of the waxy, overblown stargazer lilies. I was with you as you stood in the driving rain under unseasonal slate-grey skies while the Grief Squad (considerably cheered by the day's events, of course) flung confetti and rice at the pair of you, stinging your cheeks and loading your hair. The wind and rain hammered at the windowpanes of the gloomy Worthing hotel where we gathered to celebrate your nuptials; your guests agreed they'd never known an August like it.

During the speeches everyone drank your health and hers, the smug bitch. I wasn't referred to in person. I had become 'the past sadness' in your life. You stumbled over your words; your nose went pink at the tip. Your scrotum shrivelled when you thought of me. I danced by your side as you staggered round the floor with your bride to the cheesey strains of 'Once, Twice, Three Times a Lady'.

The marriage was consummated in our bed. Affected by Bacchanalian quantities of budget sparkling wine, you fell asleep immediately afterwards and snored. You stirred in your sleep when I whispered your name.

We honeymooned on Paxos, the three of us. You both grew fatter and redder in the sun; the retsina and oily food gave you terrible wind.

You talked about me, sometimes, in the evenings, at little restaurants with red-checked tablecloths and white candles sputtering in the sea breeze.

'Her death was meant to be,' you said. 'I can see that now.'

As you kissed across the table the flame flared up and almost scorched Sukie's hair.

You started to feel uneasy then. I stepped up the pressure. Sukie slipped and twisted her ankle climbing into a pleasure boat; you felt my fingers on your back one night in bed and your cock wilted like a stem starved of nutrients; you couldn't finish what you'd started with your new wife. You found a spray of achillea on your pillow at night, which threw Sukie into a jealous rage. And it made her sneeze. Lying on the beach turning lobster-red, you caught the scents of pine and grass cuttings and thought of me.

You started to feel guilty. You pretended to be asleep when your bride's footfall sounded across the bedroom floor.

Then you both returned to Brighton. To desecrate our home.

First Sukie ripped out our plain white units and beautiful dark worksurfaces and installed twee honeyed-pine cupboards and yellow gingham curtains. Then she polluted the living room with her prints of sunsets, her frilly cushions, her 'occasional tables'. She said our house had a stale smell, like death, and stuck plug-in airfresheners in every spare socket, like warts over skin. The garden was dying; everything choked and overgrown. She arranged for one of my old rivals to rip out the ivies and fill in the pond. She bought hideous white plastic pots and filled them with pansies.

And you didn't stop her.

She and Delia Smith kept you fat and happy as a pig in shit.

I watched your belly grow, your chest wobble, your chin sink into your neck. Sukie talked about 'starting a family' – fat little versions of the two of you running through my house, filling my once-beautiful garden with sandpits and paddling pools.

You'd acted like a bastard. You'd betrayed me. But you were only human, and despite everything, I still loved you.

I decided to rescue you.

Each night I lie between you. The new bride sleeps firmly buttoned up, slug-smug in embroidered apricot polyester. You've stopped having sex; you've told it's the pressure at work, you're too tired, you want it – when it happens – to be perfect. That one day soon things will be better. She's puzzled, hurt, she turns away from you in bed. She doesn't believe in your exhaustion, your sudden headaches. She doesn't know about the hard little tumour lodged deep in your brain, already the size of a tulip bulb. You thrash around in your dreams and I'm there, ice cold and seeking out your eyes, willing them to open.

And for a second, sweetheart, you brush my lips. And freeze.

THE BEAR

Anna lies in the dark, her eyes fixed on the cupboard door. She knows he's in there; she can hear him grunt and shuffle, lick and rasp his fur. She can smell him, too: decaying meat and leaf-mould.

Now there's a rumble, a low growl. She slides deeper under the duvet, her heart galloping. She wants to run to her mum's room but she's too terrified to move. He'll be enormous, she knows he will. He'll pounce on her the moment her feet hit the carpet; he'll tear her to shreds with his vicious claws.

She trembles for what seems like hours, wondering if she dares make a run for it. Eventually she sleeps, a light, restless sleep. She dreams she's running through the Arndale Centre in her school uniform and he's lolloping after her, and people look away, embarrassed, and nobody helps her, even though she's crying and shouting that he's going to kill her.

Next morning, when her mum comes in to wake her for school, Anna says, 'Mum, there's a bear in my cupboard.'

'What bear?' Her mum yanks the curtains open. She is already showered, her hair poker-straight and shiny, and she's dressed in a black and white fitted shirt and grey trousers. Anna can smell her vanilla body lotion and spray. She smells delicious, edible, but she seems distracted these days; she doesn't look Anna fully in the eyes.

'A really big bear,' says Anna, swinging her legs out of bed, reaching for her mother's hand.

'There's no bear and you're too old for this sort of nonsense,' says her mum, crisply. 'Go and get washed, time's getting on –'

'I can *hear* him,' says Anna. She stands up, holding her mum tightly round the waist. 'Mum, I really can...'

Her mum sighs, pushes her away and opens the cupboard door. All her dresses and tops and trousers are hanging neatly from the special wooden hangers, with board games in a pile and a few discarded dolls.

'Well, I see no bear! Where is it?' She swishes her hands through the clothes. 'It must have got bored and left. Now hurry up, darling.'

'He's gone now, he's just in there at night,' says Anna, but her mum's already on her way out and there's only the sound of her footsteps pattering down the stairs in her sheepskin slippers.

If her dad had been there he'd have looked properly for the bear. He'd have asked her about it, why she thought it was there, in her cupboard. He'd have hugged her and told her not to worry, it wouldn't hurt her. But he isn't there. He's in Scotland with his new wife and their baby and she won't see him until the summer holidays and that's five weeks away. And five weeks is a long time.

Anna eats her cereal slowly. She feels tired and numb. Her eyelids are so heavy she thinks they might keep closing and then she'll have to rest her head on her arms and go to sleep at her desk.

Her mum rushes around the kitchen, wiping surfaces, humming; bright-eyed and chipper.

'Mum,' says Anna, sucking on a strand of hair. 'Can I sleep in your room tonight?'

Her mother whisks her bowl and spoon away and stacks them in the dishwasher.

'Whatever for? And don't suck your hair.'

'The *bear*!' says Anna. 'I told you...'

'There's no bear in your cupboard. You're a big girl now. I need my sleep and you fidget. So no, absolutely not.'

Anna's throat swells and stings as though she's swallowed a bee. When she opens her mouth all that comes out is a small growl.

All morning Anna feels fuzzy and tired. She can't work out any of the answers in maths. The numbers on the whiteboard jump about. Her head throbs. At morning break she stands by the wall on her own while the other children shriek and blur past her.

After break it's art. Usually she loves art but today she's too tired. She wants to find somewhere quiet to go and sleep but she's afraid of what she might dream.

The teacher places a sheep's skull on a black cloth and gives everyone a sheet of paper and a 2B pencil.

'Look at it carefully first,' says the teacher. 'Think about shading. Work quietly and on your own, please. Twenty minutes.'

The sheep's skull is dirty white with holes where its eyes were and a grinning mouth full of big, loose teeth. She thinks it looks lonely. She doesn't want to draw it. She doesn't even want to look at it. It's dead and it seems mean to draw something dead, something that didn't ask to die and then lose its head. Some of the children make stupid noises and say, 'Ugh, Miss! Miss, it's well horrible!' The teacher tells them to settle down and stop being so silly.

Anna picks up the pencil and thinks about the bear. She knows he's real even if her mother doesn't believe in him. She closes her eyes and pictures him, clearly. She draws his dark, matted fur, shaggy head, drooping belly. She hunches over the paper, trying to get his glaring eyes just right.

'What's that?' asks the girl next to her.

'A bear. He was in my cupboard last night.'

Within minutes the whole class is in uproar: twenty-eight children gather round, jostling to see, pointing and laughing. And the teacher's clapping her hands, shouting for silence, and then saying, 'Anna, come over here. I need to talk to you. Everyone else, get on with your drawing.'

As her mother is draining the pasta for dinner, Anna tells her, 'I got into trouble today. For drawing the bear. We were meant to do a sheep's skull.'

Her mother puts down the colander and frowns. 'Drawing the *bear*?'

'Mrs Johnson wouldn't let me take it home,' says Anna, her eyes filling up. 'My drawing. I wanted to show you. But she put it in my folder. She said I was being silly.'

'Darling,' sighs her mother, tipping spaghetti on to plates, 'I really have no idea what you're talking about sometimes.'

'I'm scared of him,' says Anna. 'I really am, Mum.'

'There's nothing to be scared of,' says her mother. She spoons bolognese sauce on to the spaghetti and places a plate in front of Anna. 'It's just your imagination. Eat up, don't let it get cold...'

Steam rises off the plate into Anna's face. The sauce smells too meaty. Anna puts a little on to a spoon, then lets it slide off.

'Don't play with your food, darling,' says her mother, tucking her hair behind her ears and squaring her shoulders. 'Stop thinking about silly things and eat your dinner. You've probably read about a bear in a story and your memory is playing tricks on you, that's all.'

'I had that book about the little bear that couldn't sleep and its daddy took it out to look at the night and all the stars, but they weren't scary. They were nice bears. Daddy used to read me that one...'

'Well, there you are, then. If you imagine a bear, imagine it's a *nice* bear. A kind bear.' Her mother bites her lip and puts her fork down. 'We just have to get on with things, Anna. You're happy, aren't you? You're a happy girl?'

Anna nods. 'But could I just sleep in your bed tonight, just one night, and then I can stop thinking about the bear and then the next night he'll probably be gone, won't he?'

'No,' says her mum, sharply. 'No, I'm not starting that. Just tell yourself there's nothing there, there's nothing to be scared of, and there won't be.'

That night Anna hears the bear shifting around, the creak of its huge body rocking. The smell seems sharper, too; a smell of fresh meat and blood, like the butcher's shop her dad used to take her to on Saturday mornings while her mum was having a rest.

She hears the bear grunt. She's so frightened she's afraid she'll wet herself. She has to get out of the room. She has to get away from him.

She rolls out of bed, drops to the floor and crawls across the carpet, hardly breathing. Then she jumps up, sprints along the hall and opens her mum's door.

Her mum's bedside light is on and she's propped up against two pillows, a look of bliss on her face.

Curled on the bed is a huge male bear, asleep. His saggy belly rises and falls. His dirty brown fur is matted in places and his black, rubbery lips vibrate as he snores. He smells of meat.

'Look, darling,' her mother whispers, reaching out and stroking his huge, heavy head; he stirs slightly and grunts, and she leans over and kisses him, very gently, between the eyes. 'Isn't he beautiful? You see, silly, there's nothing to be scared of. Nothing at all.'

THE BITING POINT

'Hey, I've got it now,' says Chloe as the engine growls louder. 'I heard the clunk.'

'Good, well done. Ease off the clutch a little more... that's good... very good...'

She smiles. She knows she's looking really nice, properly fit. Her curly hair's scraped back, spiralling out of a white scrunchy, and her strappy top and combat trousers are brand new; she's a size eight, and toned, and everything fits just right. She's gone easy on the perfume – just a spray of White Musk. Nothing too overpowering in a small space; after all, you can't help sweating at times, when there's lots of traffic or the lights suddenly change. A bit sexy, but not too much; they go wild for that. He's quite old, after all, at least thirty-five, but really *cute*. And he's not wearing a wedding ring. He has long, pale hands with the neatest, cleanest fingernails ever. She's already had a dream about those hands cupping her breasts, stroking the smooth skin on her belly, like a proper lover; not like being groped by Danny Watson, with his sweaty paws...

It's a beautiful June morning, the hottest so far this year, and she's warm all over; she glances down at her arms and sees that the sun streaming through the windscreen is turning her skin a rich caramel. She wonders if he likes mixed-race girls. He looks a bit quiet, a bit shy; but he'd be mad not to want her. Loads of people have told her she's pretty enough to be a model.

'OK, so keep your hand on the handbrake, Chloe. Wait till it settles...'

Oh God, let today be the day. Today, in less than an hour's time, let him really, really want to kiss her. She's been hot for him since the first lesson, since the first handshake – weird! – on the doorstep with her mum hovering in the hallway. This is the third session and she's doing well; he's told her loads that she's doing just fine. He so obviously rates her quick brain as well as her fit body. She's a fast learner and she finds most things easy: swimming, skateboarding, ice-skating, all easy. School, exams, no sweat. She's got her six Bs and four As and her A* for drama and she's half way through 'A' levels and it's all looking good. The moment she turned seventeen she persuaded Dad to stump up for driving lessons – even if he did say that living in Streatham was hardly the back of beyond and hadn't she heard of public transport? But, like she'd told him: did he really want his daughter hanging round for buses in the middle of the night. Didn't he watch the news?

'You're incorrigible, Miss.' He'd hugged her. 'You twist me round your little finger every time...'

She grips the steering wheel now and concentrates on looking serious.

'OK, Chloe, we need to check the mirrors carefully and then the blind spots...'

She loves the way he does that exaggerated *checking* thing, craning his neck to see behind him; the way little beads of perspiration pop up on his forehead. So *caring*! She copies what he's doing, then goes back to checking the mirrors. She catches a glimpse of her face in her wing-mirror. She's looking nice. She was careful with the mascara this morning and stroked some pale-pink eye-shadow just under her brow bone to make her eyes look *really* big...

'Be aware of all these parked cars, Chloe. One might move off suddenly – remember last week, they don't always indicate...'

Yeah, yeah, she wants to say. But instead she nods, bites her lip, mutters, 'Uh-huh.'

'OK, are you happy to move off now, Chloe?'

'Very happy. Like, totally happy.'

'Fine, good. Release the handbrake, then check your mirrors once more, signal...'

Max keeps his eyes fixed on the road ahead. It's such a lovely day, he thinks, the sky bold and cloudless, all the flowers blazing in the gardens, everyone smiling and relaxed. Just hold that thought; the day is beautiful. And this girl, this Chloe, scatty drama queen though she is, will be OK as long as she keeps her eyes on the road and stops admiring herself in the mirrors.

And if he can just get through this morning, if he can just stop obsessing for long enough to bloody well teach someone to drive as he's been doing, perfectly competently, for the last ten years, without once thinking about Adam, without wanting to cry out for the touch of Adam's lips on his belly, Adam's hand clutched round his cock, he'll be fine. If he can just not think about last night. The Shiraz souring his mouth – that second bottle, always a mistake – the sudden wail of a police siren below them in the street, semen drying on his warm, damp thighs and Adam's head on his chest, weeping softly. Adam's voice, breaking up: *I can't do this any more, I just can't do this to them, this is fucking well tearing me apart...*

'Into third, Chloe,' he hears himself say, trying to keep his own voice steady. 'Gently, ease that crutch. *Clutch.*'

Shit, shit, *shit.* Crutch. Crotch. Adam's crotch. The salty sweat gleaming on his balls; their soft weight, like over-ripe plums. The damp warmth.

Damn it, she smirked a bit, looked like she was going to giggle, then stopped herself just in time. Thank God. Well, she's young, she'll probably have a laugh about it with her mates, later. When they're in some bar somewhere in the West End, off their silly heads on WKD. Oh yes, they'll all have a really good laugh about it. Never mind, move on, just focus. Keep your mind on the job, for God's sake. Forty minutes more and you can check your texts... No, don't. And don't think about him now. Don't think about the way the dark hairs around his nipples taste of wood bark. Don't think about how beautiful and pert his arse was – how you flicked your tongue over his tight buttocks – as he lay on his belly, clutching the headboard, groaning.

On the pavement are three mothers pushing bright pink and red buggies, older kids on those silver scooter things, teenage boys swaggering along with their jeans so low you can see most of their Calvin Klein underwear; the outline of high, tight arses. The black boys in particular move so easily, like dancers, like dolphins. They seem to own the pavement with their easy grace, their confidence. They are entitled. Anyone under thirty feels so completely entitled; not yet bogged down with wrong choices, bills, love that won't shift...

Don't think this stuff, just stop it. Focus. Concentrate.

The girl is driving too fast; she's too confident already, too full of herself. Teenage girls like this make him nervous; everything about them is too much – they're too physical, too in-your-face. He prefers teaching the quiet, serious ones, the ones with spots and glasses. This little minx will probably shag her boyfriend straight after the lesson.

'Coming up to the junction with the main road, now, Chloe,' he says. 'You should be in second. Ease down now – nice and smooth...'

'OK, cool,' she twitters, crunching the gears, and the car whines as it slows down behind a motorbike. It ticks in the heat.

Cool. He hates that word.

Despite the blast from the air-conditioning, Chloe's hands are sweating. Her left foot, in its bright white trainer, hovers over the clutch, trembling. She stares straight ahead and wishes she'd brought some sunglasses – one, they'd make her look even better; two, she wouldn't be squinting into this fucking sun like a moron...

Crutch. He said crutch. He so did. Definitely. Oh my God, does this mean he actually fancies her, is he thinking of them, naked, in bed together?

She's flushing. Shit. *Stay cool*, she thinks, *just stay ice cool.*

She's never been completely naked with a man before. With Danny, she's taken her top off, let him feel her tits a bit. On his birthday she let him suck her nipples, though she didn't enjoy it – he slurped, which was gross, and had sharp teeth so they felt sore and chapped afterwards. And he's slid his hand down her knickers a few times when they were watching DVDs in his bedroom, and rummaged around as if he'd lost something. And she's tugged his dick once or twice in a half-hearted way after he begged her to – no way was she going any further than that. But she's never wanted to see him naked, not really. He's OK, but he's not exactly hot. With Max she's already imagined what he'll look like. He's taller than Danny, slimmer, with that brownish-fair hair – maybe quite a hairy chest...

'Down into first, Chloe, ease that clutch up now, you're still a bit fast – it's quite a busy junction...'

Her knees piston up and down. She brings the car to a stop and yanks up the handbrake as the vehicles pant in the heat like a row of dogs waiting for water. The sun is wicked today. It bounces off the cars' paintwork, blinding. Sun makes people hornier, their hormones go crazy; it's been proved, loads of times. People have more sex in the summer. The traffic stretches back along Nimrod Road. She's driving past her old primary school; this is her territory, and now she's moving on. She wonders if anyone recognises her: little Chloe Shadbolt, always so pretty and neat, and now she's in this cute Corsa being taught to drive by this man. She hopes someone *will* see her. Not Danny – that would be a pain, he'd wave and distract her – but maybe some of her mates.

She says 'Phew!' and smiles at Max, and he smiles back. Shyly. He looks away, quickly; that's a sign, she's sure it's a sign.

And now he's looking out of the side window, a bit distracted. He's probably feeling a bit guilty because she's so young. Maybe he's got a girlfriend but she'll be a drag, some boring woman who's starting to look *old*, someone he's been going out with for ages and can't bring himself to ditch...

'We're going right here, Chloe, not left. Check around you, check your mirrors, indicate...'

Right. They've never turned right here before. Maybe he's planning to take her past his flat? Maybe he'll even get her to park outside. Maybe he'll say, 'By the way, this is where I live.' He won't ask her in today, but he'll just let her know...

'Ease out gently, keep looking, keep going, nice and smooth. This is a busy road, remember, that's fine, that's good...'

He *so* fancies her. It's obvious. She slips the car back into second gear and it's effortless, smooth; the engine sounds happy.

'How was that?' she asks, almost laughing.

'That was fine, Chloe, that was very good. Ease up into third...'

God, he's sexy. That voice. The lovely soft edges to his words. Everything he says is sexy. In bed he'd be in control, he'd know what to do. 'Chloe,' he'd say, 'you're so, so beautiful.' And he wouldn't go too fast, she's sure of that. He'd kiss her loads first, all over...

'We're going to be turning right again when we come to Idle-combe Road. It's the next on the right, after Salterford, so be pre-pared to indicate, back into second, slow down here...'

She runs her tongue over her top lip. There's a steady stream of traffic in the other lane; lots of those stupid Chelsea tractors full of stressed-out women driving their horrible kids to ballet and tai chi and all that shit. And boys with stereos so loud the whole thing throbs, the saddoes. She'll show him how cool she is about all this, how competent. She indicates, glides into a space, and they sit there with the indicator ticking and she knows he's admiring the way she's staying so sorted.

And then, for no reason, the car stalls. It dies. She's sitting there and the engine's sputtered to a stop and the fucking thing's dead. She's hot all over, twisting the ignition key, fumbling with the gear stick, trying to find neutral.

'Stay calm, don't worry. You just needed a bit more accelera-tor. Find first, then put the clutch right down, that's it, then bring it up slowly, slowly... a little more gas... that's it, that's good, find the biting point... got it?'

'Got it!' she shouts, and they both laugh and then there's a space in the traffic as a man in a crappy old Lada is kind and flashes his lights at them, and she can do the turn. She swings the car smoothly into the quieter side street and he says, 'Great, well done.'

And suddenly she imagines his tongue on her breast and his teeth sinking in, ever so gently, and maybe just biting her a little bit, just nipping the skin, and she breathes out through her lips, slowly. It feels lovely and she grips the wheel tighter.

He'll get her to do a three-point turn: this road is quiet with enough spaces on either side. It has to be done and at least it uses up time and she can't go too fast; she's obviously a bit keen on speed, this one. She'll end up in some souped-up chickmobile daddy buys for her, screeching along Streatham High Road in the early hours, hip-hop blasting from the speakers. But that's not his problem; just get her through this, just teach her how to do it. Please God don't her let her cock this up; concentrating is hard enough today.

'We're going to pull in over there, Chloe. There's a nice big space so just slow down, indicate, pull in – and then turn off the engine.'

He drifts for a few moments, closes his eyes as the girl feeds the wheel through her hands; he should be reminding her to check her mirrors but he finds he's remembering the first time he and Adam kissed. Their third date – though Adam would never call them dates; he'd always say, 'We're just two blokes going out for a pint.' But dates, that's what they were. Two people falling for each other, unable to keep from touching each other. A long, slow kiss in a Soho basement bar on a dismally wet November night, both their jackets still steaming slightly, a bored-looking barman arranging glasses in the corner. Adam's mouth so open and wet and the kiss so long and lazy, their tongues mingling so effortlessly it was as if their bodies had fused. That was the night Adam had said, 'OK, yes, I want this. This is what I want. I want to stay married, I want to be a good dad to Jack, but I can't not kiss you...'

And then they'd touched each other's faces and he'd ruffled Adam's hair and stroked behind his ears. He'd loved feeling in control, at that moment; Adam hadn't done this before, he said, or not for years, not since he was a student and got drunk and he and a mate had ended up in bed together. He'd pressed his hand on Adam's leg and Adam had made a little noise, like a kitten waking up; and then they kissed some more – and that night...

Six months ago, and now Adam's saying enough. *I can't do this. Please just leave, please just get out of my life before anyone else gets hurt.* A few short hours ago. He hadn't meant it; when Max texted him first thing this morning he got straight back with, *I love you*

2, always will. So juvenile, really, this texting thing, but it turned him on just the same; once, when he was drunk, he'd texted Adam a photo of himself in the bath and Adam had...

She's parked, without talking, thank God. Not bad, actually: more or less parallel with the kerb and plenty of space front and back and she's turned off the engine and is sitting nice and demure, not sneaking glances at herself in the mirror. And the sun's less of a problem in this road; more shade.

Better get on with this. Better concentrate.

He smiles at her, hoping his boredom doesn't show, and she smiles back. She's keen, anyway. She wants to pass this test first time so she can get on with impressing her friends in her chickmobile.

'Well done,' he says. 'And do you know what I'm going to ask you to do now?'

Chloe shakes her head; she tries to speak but her lips won't open. She's never felt this churned up before, this sense of being in someone's power. Usually she's the one who calls the shots – the adored, not the adoring, the one who dishes out favours. Her knickers are so damp she feels she might stick to the seat. This could be it. He might want to kiss her now, in the car, in the street. He might not be able to hold off any longer.

'We need to do the three-point turn here. It's officially called the turning in the road, using forward and reverse gears. You know about that from your theory test, right?'

Shit. She's going to have to concentrate and it's so hard, she was so sure he'd...

'Right,' she says. She smiles as brightly as she can. She can't really remember what you have to do for a three-point turn. Something about full locks and then turning the wheel back again and ending up over the other side of the road and not going over the kerb. The theory test was weeks ago and anyway it was just like school: you learn stuff, do a test, pass it, forget it. She needs to manage it properly, though. She needs to show him she's a good driver, that the stalling thing was just a blip...

'Let's go through what you need to do, shall we?' He pushes his hair back from his forehead. She loves those dark eyebrows, and the eyes – somewhere between grey and green. Seriously cute.

'Cool.' Shit, her voice sounds like a mouse-squeak, not a sexy woman. She clears her throat and tucks a stray hair behind her ear.

'So, to start, turn on the engine, check all around you for traffic and pedestrians...'

He's so calm, so sorted. She'll show him she can do this. She'll get this right first time.

'Check your mirrors, signal right, don't start turning the wheel until the car moves forward. Then right hand down – clockwise, move out nice and slowly, checking your mirrors. *Hard* down on the wheel, Chloe – we need full lock here...'

She inches the car forward until it's half way across the road. Max is making really nice, encouraging noises and it's all fine. She likes the feeling of being half way across the road, and everything being slow, and Max saying, 'Hard down, Chloe' which makes her a bit shivery as she imagines her legs wide apart and him slamming into her so hard she's breathless, speechless. Then she sees there's a white van waiting to drive down the road and the driver – a big shaven-haired guy chewing gum – is looking bored. Well, fuck him.

'OK, now when you get to about two thirds of the way across – that's it, that's good – start moving the wheel back in the opposite direction – so your wheels are straightening – that's good – not too fast – so that you're nearing the opposite kerb...'

He's excited. She knows he's wound up because there's sweat gleaming on his upper lip. Any minute now and this stupid turn thing will be over and he'll say, *well done, clever girl.* And then, for sure, he'll pretend he's just patting her knee supportively and then she won't stop him and he'll give her leg a long, slow squeeze...

And then suddenly the white-van man blasts his horn, twice, and the air rips open and somehow her foot slips and then the car shoots forward and out of nowhere there's a little boy running along the pavement, a very blonde boy in a blue stripy T-shirt, about three, with his face all lit up and open and the car lurches forward and veers on to the pavement and she screams and everything freezes, she can't stop this happening. And Max's face is rigid, all the colour drained out, and he's slamming on the dual-control brake and shouting...

'You stupid, stupid little bitch! For God's sake, you could have killed him... for God's sake...'

Max yanks the handbrake up, shaking. He feels sick. On the pavement the kid is crying – his mouth a huge, inconsolable 'O' of fear and shock. The mother has wrapped him in her arms and is stroking his hair. As Adam's wife would, if that boy were Jack. She would be comforting him now, her heart hammering in her chest, and hating the idiots in the car who'd nearly ploughed into him, left him mashed, bloodied, on the pavement.

An unforgivable thing to do. A moment's carelessness and everything changes: one moment it's a beautiful spring morning in a South London suburb and the next it's all blood, hospitals, pain.

The white-van man is still blasting his horn, the stupid bastard. Max wants to punch his lights out. A little knot of people – women and kids – are gathering round the boy and his mother.

He has to deal with this. He steps on to the pavement and the woman turns on him, her face a snarl.

'She could have run him down! She could have killed him! You should have stopped her – '

'I put the brakes on the moment I could,' he says, trying to keep his voice low and calm. 'It was a genuine mistake on her part, she just slipped. Is your little boy all right? Are you all right?'

'Just go,' the woman hisses, picking up the whimpering boy as the crowd around them closes in, clucking disapproval. Max's face is burning. He's never understood before how it must feel to have that much adrenalin coursing through your veins, to experience that primal rush of fury.

'Just fuck off out of here,' the woman says over her shoulder as she walks away with her child, his head flopping on her shoulder. 'And tell that stupid little cow she's no business driving if she can't do it right.'

He opens the driver's door. The girl is still sobbing, her face in her hands; noisy, gulping sobs.

'Get out of the car, Chloe,' he says as calmly as he can. 'I'm going to take you home.'

She turns to him, her face a blotched mess of snot and smudged mascara. She looks about twelve, suddenly; a frightened kid. She just sits there, snivelling.

He clears his throat. Adam, naked, crying. *I can't do this. I can't do this to them.*

'I'm sorry I shouted,' he says, crouching down beside her. 'I shouldn't have done that, I was shocked and reacted badly. I'm sorry. But Chloe, you need to get out of the car, we're causing an obstruction here...'

White-van man hoots again, as do several cars behind him. Max feels strangely calm; beyond caring. As Chloe unclips her seatbelt he notices her hands are shaking and pats them. Then she leans over and wraps her arms around his neck and buries her face in his chest.

He feels paralysed, revolted; she's a damp, needy heap, clinging to him. He rubs her shoulders, awkwardly, and she clings tighter. He unpeels her arms.

'Chloe,' he says coldly, 'please get out of the car and we'll get you home. You'll feel better soon, I promise.'

She lifts her face to him. Poor kid.

The air is full of drivers' horns and swearing. The day is shattered, he thinks; all the blue sky and heat, wasted. Now all that's left is to clear up the mess. He won't contact Adam to say goodbye. He'll change his SIM card, get a new number. That will be kinder. Walk away. Adam will become a memory in time, a married-man memory. A man with a wife and son and the life he's chosen, and no more secrets and lies and no more of his illicit, beautiful body.

He takes Chloe's hand and leads her round to the passenger seat and clips her in. Breathing slowly and steadily he settles himself in the driver's seat and switches on the engine. He pushes the clutch down hard and then lets it up gently, pressing the accelerator, giving it just enough gas; just enough power to get going.

ACKNOWLEDGEMENTS

are due to the editors of *Quality Women's Fiction*, *Cadenza*, *Buzz Words*, *Writer's Express*, the Hastings Writers' Group anthologies and *Dreamcatcher*, in which some of these stories were first published. Warm thanks also to the Arvon Foundation at Totleigh Barton and to Ruary OSiochain for great spaces to write, and to Ros Barber, Sarah Salway, Kerrith Etkin-Bell, Gaye Gee, Umi Sinha, Jackie Hinden, Felicity Napier, Carol Rowe, Kevin Parry, Trevor Pateman, Peter Abbs, Julia Widdows, Lorna Thorpe, Clare Best, Monique Roffey and Mark Hewitt for support, advice, criticism and wine. Special thanks to Vicky Wilson at Categorical Books for her editing skills and general brilliance.

Three of the stories in this collection, 'Sow', 'The Kettle' and 'The Ascension of Mary', have been adapted for a Live Literature/stage performance, *Weight*, under the direction of Mark Hewitt at Lewes Live Literature. For further details, please go to www.leweslivelit.co.uk.

CATHERINE SMITH

was born and grew up in Windsor. She started writing poetry and stories when she was seven, carried on until she was a teenager, won a few prizes and then gave up her own work to concentrate on other (more famous) people's as she studied for her first degree, in Literature/History of Ideas and History, at Bradford University. She studied Creative Writing at Sussex University at MA level when her children were young and soon had poems and stories accepted for publication in literary magazines and anthologies. In 2004 she was included in both *Mslexia*'s 'Top Ten Women Poets' selection and in the PBS/Arts Council 'Next Generation' promotion. Two of her poetry collections, *The Butcher's Hands* and *Lip* (Smith/Doorstop Books, 2003 and 2007), have been shortlisted for the Forward Prize and her short stories have won prizes in local and national competitions. She lives in East Sussex and teaches Creative Writing for Sussex University, Varndean Sixth Form College and the Arvon Foundation. This is her first full collection of stories.

For more information about Catherine and her work, go to:
www.speechbubblebooks.co.uk
www.catherinesmithwriter.co.uk
www.leweslivelit.co.uk

Lightning Source UK Ltd.
Milton Keynes UK
UKOW032245091012

200325UK00001B/60/P